Thomas Widd

The Deaf and Dumb and Blind Deaf-Mute

With Interesting Facts and Anecdotes - a short history of the MacKay

Institution - an easy method of teaching deaf-mutes at home

Thomas Widd

The Deaf and Dumb and Blind Deaf-Mute
*With Interesting Facts and Anecdotes - a short history of the MacKay Institution -
an easy method of teaching deaf-mutes at home*

ISBN/EAN: 9783337392741

Printed in Europe, USA, Canada, Australia, Japan

Cover: Foto ©Andreas Hilbeck / pixelio.de

More available books at **www.hansebooks.com**

THE

Deaf and Dumb

AND

BLIND DEAF-MUTES,

WITH INTERESTING FACTS AND ANECDOTES; A SHORT
HISTORY OF THE MACKAY INSTITUTION; AN EASY
METHOD OF TEACHING DEAF-MUTES AT HOME;
THE AUDIPHONE, ETC.

———

ILLUSTRATED BY DEAF-MUTE ARTISTS,

———

A COMPILATION BY
THOMAS WIDD,
Principal of the Mackay Institution for Protestant Deaf-mutes, Montreal.

————◦————

MONTREAL:
F. E. GRAFTON, PUBLISHER, 252 ST. JAMES STREET.
——
1880.

MONTREAL :

PRINTED BY THE BOYS AT THE MACKAY INSTITUTION FOR PROTESTANT DEAF-MUTES.

COTE ST. LUC ROAD.

TO THE MANY KIND FRIENDS
OF THE
DEAF AND DUMB
THIS LITTLE WORK IS MOST
RESPECTFULLY AND GRATEFULLY
DEDICATED.

TO THE READER.

HAVING suffered from the most intense deafness for more than thirty-five years, and labored as a teacher and missionary to the deaf and dumb for twenty years, the Compiler of this little work is, in consequence, thoroughly acquainted with the requirements of this afflicted class. He would urge all who possess any influence, however small, with our *Legislators*, to use that influence to obtain for the deaf-mute, in the name of humanity and justice, the *same facilities for education and spiritual instruction as are enjoyed by persons who can hear and speak.* He wants justice, not charity. There is no class of people in the world who have been so much misunderstood, who have had to contend with so many difficulties and hardships, and whose motives have been so often mistaken as the DEAF AND DUMB; and on this account the compiler has always striven, and still strives, to ameliorate their condition and to obtain for them their just rights. His humble efforts in this direction, in England and Canada, have, thanks to a kind Providence and to Christian benevolence, been attended with some success. But the education of this class in Canada is yet in its infancy. More schools (*not asylums*) are wanted (each containing not more than 20 to 100 pupils), also a college for higher education, and places for divine service in the finger and sign-language in towns and cities. The deaf-mute, when properly instructed and trained, is not altogether helpless, as will be seen from this little book,—the type-setting, printing, and the engraving of nearly all the illustrations having been executed by deaf and dumb workmen.

PREFACE.

THERE is a great want of correct knowledge respecting the affliction of deafness, particularly as regards its fearful consequences. Very few persons, even among the thoughtful and intelligent, are fully acquainted with the natural and moral state of the deaf and dumb, the condition of their minds, the peculiar means employed in their education, and the nature of their employments in after life. The consequences of deafness are constantly confounded with those of blindness in the minds of many for want of a little careful considera-tion of the essential difference between them. Another error is to regard the deaf and dumb as little, if at all, better than idiots. Many other mistakes might be mentioned, but as they are dealt with in the body of this work, it will be unnecessary to refer to them here.

These misapprehensions concerning this afflicted class, coupled with the apparent mysteriousness which is attached to the mode of their instruction, show how necessary it is that correct information on the subject should be diffused as widely as possible, that the consequences of this deprivation may be better under-stood and realized, and that the benevolent projects established for their welfare may receive the full benefit of an *enlightened* sympathy.

With a view to diffuse as widely as possible much general information respecting this class and to correct prevailing errors respecting them, this little work has been issued. The materials have been gathered from over twenty years' practical experience amongst the deaf and dumb, both children and adults, in Europe and Canada. Extracts have been made from the works of other writers, especially from " Language by Touch," by Mr. Wallis, which refers chiefly to the blind deaf-mutes; and " The Deaf and Dumb," by the Rev. S. Smith, London. The history of the Mackay Institution, and an easy method of teaching deaf-mutes at home are here introduced, mainly to encourage others in their efforts to start similar schools wherever required.

It has been the aim to make these pages interesting and instructive to both young and old. The writer is himself a deaf-mute, and, having derived so much benefit from instruction is most anxious that all deaf-mutes should enjoy similar advantages. Any profits arising from the sale of the book will be used to help to ameliorate the condition of the children of silence.   T. W.

Montreal, January, 1880.

CONTENTS.

viii.

CHAPTER XI.

CHAPTER XII.

LIST OF ILLUSTRATIONS.

THE DEAF AND DUMB.

CHAPTER I.

The Early Dawn—London—Paris—Hartford.

ONE fine day in the month of May, 1662, there was a large assembly of great persons in Whitehall, London. His Majesty Charles I. was there, surrounded by nobles and fair ladies, by diplomatists and bishops, learned men of all kinds, and ambassadors from foreign lands. The thoroughfare leading to Whitehall was crowded with carriages and horses, and people on foot. Presently there appeared before the King and his grand assembly a learned doctor and profound philosopher, named John Wallis, who led by the hand a little boy, and all eyes were directed to them. There was nothing extraordinary in their appearance, and most of the people present wondered what was going to be done. No king was going to be crowded; no royal marriage was to be solemnized; no unfortunate culprit was to be executed,—then why this grand gathering? Dr. Wallis had been invited to exhibit before the King his triumphant achievement in having successfully instructed a deaf-mute! He had taught him to read and write, and the world wondered! His name was Daniel Whalley.

Let us cross the English Channel, and see what was being done for the deaf-mute in Paris about a century after Dr. Wallis's time. A benevolent-looking gentleman in the garb of a Roman Catholic priest, the Abbe L'Epee, was wending his way through the thronged streets of Paris to make his usual round of visits. In one house dwelt a lady and her two daughters, whom the good Abbe visited. He entered a room in which the two young ladies were seated at needlework. No response was made to his salutation, which much surprised him. In explanation of this apparent rudeness, he learned that these two lovely young ladies were both deaf and dumb. The Abbe's kind heart was touched to the quick, and he resolved to devote the remainder of his existence to their education. He soon found that there were many others similarly afflicted, and to devise means by which to reach their imprisoned minds became his sole thought day and night. His efforts were not in vain, for he soon found a way, by signs and gestures and the one-handed alphabet, to convey instruction to the children of silence in his country. He afterwards founded the institution for deaf-mutes at Paris

We now cross the broad Atlantic and come nearer home. Towards the close of the last century, in a pleasant home near New Haven, Conn., a little girl was born deaf and dumb, and a few years after a second daughter was born, and she, alas! was found to be deaf and dumb also. It was a bitter trial to the Christian parents of these afflicted children, and they wondered why a loving God should afflict them so sorely. These little girls grew up to be beautiful young women. They were ladies in manner, but totally uninstructed. The Rev. T. H. Gallaudet had recently returned from Europe where he had learned how to teach deaf-mutes and founded the school for them at Hartford. These girls were then in their teens, and their parents hastened with them to Mr. Gallaudet. They were among those who formed his first class of deaf-mutes. The youngest made great progress in her studies, and when she completed her education became the wife and co-laborer of this distinguished gentleman. She bore him eight children, one of whom is the Principal of the present National College for Deaf-mutes at Washington, and another is the Rev. Dr. Gallaudet, of St. Ann's Church for Deaf-mutes, in New York.

CHAPTER II.

The Single and Double Handed Alphabets and their Advantages.

Now to return to Dr. Wallis. We find that he used a double-handed alphabet in teaching his first pupil, and this alphabet was invented by a very learned philosopher, named George Delgarno, a Scotchman by birth, who now lies in a nameless grave in St. Mary's Churchyard, Oxford, England.

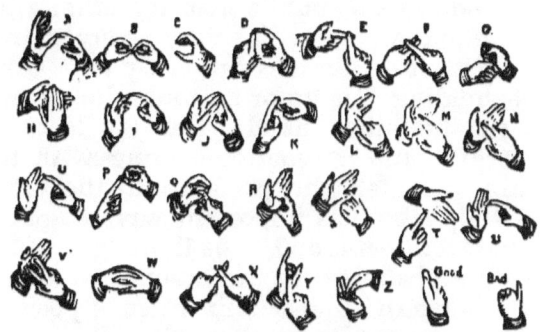

THE TWO-HANDED ALPHABET.

Delgarno wrote a valuable book about teaching deaf and dumb persons, but Wallis was the first to carry the idea of teaching them into practical effect. The vowels of this alphabet are formed by touching the tips of the fingers of the left hands with the index finger of the other. It it used in all the schools for deaf-mutes in Great Britain and other countries to this day.

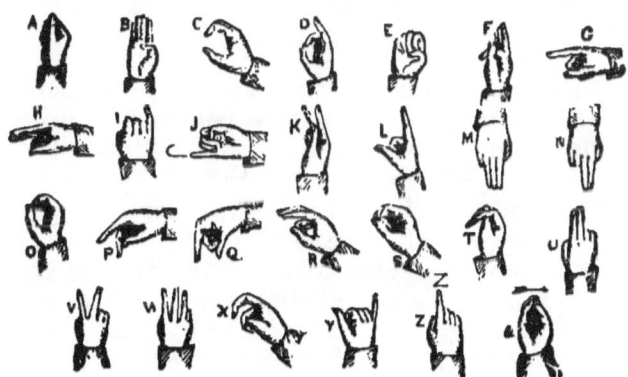

THE ONE-HANDED ALPHABET.

The one-handed alphabet used by Abbe L'Epee is different from the above. It was in use before his time. It is employed in the schools for deaf-mutes in the United States and France. The alphabet made with the two hands has a strong resemblance to the capital letters of the Roman Alphabet, while the one-handed alphabet bears a likeness to script, and on these accounts both alphabets can be very easily learned and remembered. The two-handed alphabet is more distinct and is far better known and more generally used by the public than the other alphabet. The one-handed alphabet is very convenient and graceful. With it deaf-mutes can carry on a conversation while holding a lamp or an umbrella, or book, or the reins in the other hand. But for lecturing or religious service, and for communicating with hearing and speaking people, who prefer it to the other, the two-handed alphabet has important advantages. It is therefore best for deaf-mutes to be thoroughly acquainted with both alphabets. In the practice of either it is necessary to keep in mind certain rules of position, for on these their perspicuity depends. In using the double-handed alphabet the left hand should be held open in front of the person addressed, and the fingers of the right hand should travel over the left hand making the letters distinctly and deliberately. The skilful dactylologist is able to speak with the rapidity of ordinary speech, and any one able to read and write will soon become expert with either alphabet after a little patience and perseverance. The reader can study them both and compare their respective merits at his leisure.

CHAPTER III.

The Uneducated Deaf-mute—The Sign-Language— The Difficulties in the Acquisition of Language —The Deaf-mute's and the Armenian's Letters. —From the Creature to the Creator.

With these alphabets the instruction of deaf-mutes became more general. Schools for them were established in most civilized countries. They became the key to the minds of these afflicted ones, and a kind of substitute for the potent "Ephphatha!" But to educate the deaf-mute appalling difficulties have to be surmounted. He knows *no language*, except a few gestures and simple signs. It is difficult for those not deaf to conceive of ideas without language. The most uncivilized savage has a language, and can express his ideas to those speaking his language. So the deaf-mute, until he acquires a knowledge of language, expresses his ideas in natural signs and gestures—the same as infants use. When a deaf-mute goes to a school for deaf and dumb children, his teacher has to supply both thought and language, and then to lay out and cultivate the many avenues to the mind over which thought goes and comes. His lessons involve much translation—first emotion into ideas, ideas into signs, and signs into written words, or words spelled out by the fingers letter for letter. Constant repetition is necessary to fix the words in the mind. The great difficulty is to get him to understand and remember *words enough to convey his ideas* as he writes or converses with hearing and speaking people. We now realize how much a child blessed with the gift of hearing and speech knows of language when he first goes to school—he has been taught by all the people he ever met by simply *hearing them speak.* But the only preparation the deaf-mute has received when he goes to school is his careful observation of the motions and behavior of people and things about him,

The difficulties besetting the progress of the deaf-mute are chiefly in the way of language. His means of expressing his wants and emotions are those which Darwin has shown to be common with the brute creation. His pantomimes are no more like words than is the chatter of birds or the grimaces of a monkey. When his motions have been directed into the defined expression of thought his signs indicate ideas rather than the arbitrary symbols of speech. He has none of the benefits of comparative philology. All spoken language have certain semblances by which, knowing one language, the acquisition of others is facilitated. Yet, M. Hamerton, is his "Intellectual Life," says: "A language cannot be thoroughly learned by an adult without five years residence in the country where it is spoken, and without close observation, a residence of twenty years is insufficient." This is not encouraging, but it is the truth. What then shall be expected of a deaf-mute, whose only opportunities for the acquirement of the English language are limited to the formulas of the class-room and occasional conversations with intelligent friends by pen or pencil? The first six or seven years in a deaf-mute's school life should be devoted to the study of language,—to obtain the key that unlocks to him the stores of human learning as contained in books. In this pursuit it is not the hundred thousand words of the dictionary that confuse the pupils, and dishearten the teacher, but the different uses to which the same words are put, and the differeut ideas depending simply on conjunction. Take, as a simple illustration, the word "draw." The pupil is taught that a horse draws a waggon. The pantomime is clear and corresponds with his daily observation. But to his surprise, the next morning's paper, in its notices, says: "The concert drew a large house last night," and he has to learn that in this use draw means to attract, and house means a number of people. After being taught by pantomime to draw a picture. He is told if he is ever so fortunate as to have money on deposit, he must draw a check before he can get it. He has seen a school-mate draw a picture, but when the heroine of a modern novel "draws a sigh," his admiration for the capacity of art is increased. A magazine criticism commends the scenes of innocence and content which Milton "draws," but on reference to the parlor edition of "Paradise Lost," he finds no illustrations, or only those which Gustave Dore has made. One must confess that the pupil has enough already to confuse him, but when, in addition, he is told that "a ship draws water," "a cook draws a fowl," "a waiter draws a cork," "money draws interest," and "a minister draws comparisons and references," he concludes in despair that the conundrums of language are things which no deaf-mute can find out. When to these numerous significations the modifying adverbs in, out, off, on, up, back, etc., are added, and when it is remembered that every peculiar use of a word must be made a special subject of instruction and retained by a special effort of memory, a keyhole perception may be obtained of the work involved in the education of a deaf-mute.

To illustrate the natural language of signs of the deaf and dumb in order that the reader may better understand it, let us suppose, for instance, that an uneducated deaf-mute had witnessed a drunken man run over by a carriage and carried to the hospital or to his house, he would run home in a state of excitement, arrest his mother's attention, make the sign he had been using for man (probably by referring to his beard and showing his height), and then imitate his staggering gait as he went along : afterwards describing the galloping of a horse and the revolving of wheels as approaching the man, showing the shape of the vehicle as well as he could. He would then represent the man as being knocked down by it, showing over what part of the man's body they passed over by touching the part of his own. He would then make the sign for more men by holding up his fingers to denote the number; point to the door or shutter to describe the stretcher on which the injured man was carried, and imitating the carrying of something heavy on his shoulder, and the moving away of the crowd, by waving his hand in one direction. But he would not be able to tell the name of the street or place where this occurred, nor the name of the man injured, or that of the owner of the carriage ;—nor would he be able to state anything that the people might have said about the affair, or any other details which a little hearing and speaking child would have been able to do. With such language the deaf-mute is unable to tell his own name or that of any of his friends, but he generally has signs for each by which he indicates them; and this sign is taken from prominent features in their appearance or action, viz., pointing to the place of the wedding ring for his mother, the whiskers for father, and indicating the several heights for his brothers and sisters; limping to indicate some lame friend, and the sharpening of the knife for the butcher. It will thus be seen that the deaf-mute needs *a language common to those around him* by which he can communicate with the world. This is the greatest difficulty in deaf-mute instruction and requires years of toil, patience and perseverance. He learns everything through the EYE, not by the *ear*. The first year at school is generally spent in teaching nouns and phrases and a little of arithmetic. The second year he goes over the same nouns and phrases and learn to combine words into sentences. Most intelligent deaf-mutes can write a few sentences to express their ideas, or write a short letter to their friends, after being two or three years at school.

The following is the uncorrected letter from a boy deaf and dumb from infancy after being *three years* in the Protestant (now Mackay) Institution for Deaf-mutes, at Montreal:—

"I received your very kind letter from you and was glad to hear from you and know that you are getting better now. My father told me will go to Montreal next September 3rd. I will be glad to see you and your family. I went to the mines last Tuesday. There was a man kill, he fell forty feet at the mines. The men are working the mines. It is rainy now. I am very busy. The crop is good, the plums is plenty. My cousin and me will mow the oats soon. I think you will go to New York one week. I am happy with my parents at home. I send my love to you."

The writer of this article received another letter from a converted Armenian Mohammedan who had been spending *eight* years at a college in the United States learning the English language. The Armenian understood and used his native language, for he was not deaf and dumb. We will compare his letter with that of the deaf-mute's. It will help to give some idea of their difficulties in learning the English language. The Armenian had recently visited Montreal, and his impressions of the city and the people are curious:

"I am going Hamilton College, N. Y. Where am studying to return home Armenia, as I told you when your kind hospitality I was enjoying. I shook 3 times the dust of my foot just now against thise city, and again my brethren who herd me lest night in praree meating I return my censer thank for loving kindness. 'I was a sturenger you took me in.' The Lord give you helthe to teach blessed Gospele to those who are unabl to hear yet Jesus Chrest dide for them for me and for aney bodey. Bible sed ' what me sow the same will me reap.' If I was verey rech the hall city would respect me. If I had nice dresses, stofe-pofe hat rengs on my fenger golden wach and chane and $. certainlly I could lechur on Koran and Mohammedanism. Brethren find plenety excuses just as faresees had when they sow the merecals which our Lord performe."

It is easy to teach a deaf-mute how to write, but a very different thing to get him to understand what he writes or what is written to him Parents and teachers in public schools often make mistakes in attempting to teach little deaf and dumb children without any knowledge of the proper way. Once a schoolmaster brought a little deaf-mute boy to an institution for deaf-mutes in England, and said he had already taught him some useful knowledge. He was asked what he had taught him. He said he had taught him to know that "the way of God was a good way." He was asked to show how he knew the boy understood the sentence, and he made the boy copy it. This was to him sufficient proof, but he had never tried to explain to the boy either what *God was*, or what the *way of God* was. It would be a long time before a good teacher of deaf-mutes would bring such a sentence for his pupil to understand. He would explain to him something of the nature of the Almighty, when the pupil could understand the language necessary to express it, and then the *way of God* would still have to be explained as a metaphorical expression. To teach a deaf-mute an idea of a Supreme Being who is called "God," the teacher would begin thus: A desk is before the pupil. He asks him, "Who made it?" "A man—a carpenter." "Of what is it made?" "Of wood." "Did man make the wood?" "No." "Where did he get it from?" "Trees." "Did man make the trees?" "No; they grow." "How?" "By the sun, rain, &c." "Does man make the sun shine and the rain to fall?" "No." "*Who does?*" They must be told that it is GOD who does all these things. So on step by step, from the works of man to the works of God, and from the creature to the Creator.

Lessons on secular subjects come in their turn— geography, history, arithmetic, &c: but the great aim of the teacher is to give them a knowledge of ordinary language that they may understand what they read, and to be able to write down their thoughts for others not able to understand their signs and the finger language. Many of them do learn to write down their thoughts in correct language, and some of them learn to talk and read people's lips when they are spoken to orally.

B

CHAPTER IV.

Anecdotes of Deaf-mutes.—A Deaf-mute's Prayer.—
The Finger and Sign-Language Utilized.—"Jesus
and Me."—Deaf-mute Artists.—A Prodigy.—Deaf-
mute Compositions.—Massieu and Clerc.—Absurd
Expectations.

It would tire the reader to follow the deaf-mute
through all the stages of his instruction at school, and
it will perhaps be more pleasant to read a few anecdotes
of deaf-mutes that have lived since the days of good
Dr. Wallis and his early co-laborers

About fifty years ago, Lord Seaforth, who was born
deaf and dumb, was to dine one day with Lord Melville
in London. Just before the company arrived- Lady
Melville sent a lady who could talk on her fingers to
meet Lord Seaforth and talk to him. Lord
Guilford, who was not deaf and dumb, entered
before Lord Seaforth, and the lady mistook him for the
dumb lord, and entered into conversation with him on
her fingers. He did the same. After a few minutes
Lady Melville came into the room, and the lady said
to her, " Well, I have been talking away to this dumb
man." " Dumb!" exclaimed Lord Guilford, " Bless me,
I thought you were dumb!"

The following prayer was written by a deaf-mute
boy named Joseph Turner of Edinburgh, who became a
teacher of deaf-mutes, and was used by himself, because,
as he said, he wanted to become a good man:

"O God, take pity on me; bless me; forgive me my sin, for I am a poor
guilty sinner; keep me from neglecting to think much of thee, and of
Jesus Christ, and to pray to Thee. Give me wisdom of Thyself to think
attentively how to pray to Thee. Oh! I thank Thee, for Thou hast given
my master wisdom to teach me and my dear poor companions about the
religion of Thee and of Jesus Christ. Oh! pardon my sin; give me wisdom
to understand surely what he says about religion. Oh! give me good
care not to break the Sabbath day, but earnestly to read in the life of Christ.
O God, open my mind surely to understand what I read in it. Oh! I
would thank Thee to give my companions wisdom to understand what
they read. Oh! hear me! Thou art God; besides Thee there is no Saviour.
Thou art holy. Oh! make me to hate sin, and to love the good! Oh!
give me grace to glorify Thee! Save me from hell; take me to Jesus
Christ when I die. O Lord for the Sake of Christ, wilt Thou hear me?
O God, give me good thoughts from heaven through Jesus Christ. I thank

Thee that we are at peace in all the world, in They presence. Make us obedient to Thee and Jesus Christ Thy Son, in believing the gospel, and reading the Holy Bible concerning Thee and Him. O God, maker of heaven and earth, I look toward heaven. Forgive me my sin, for I have committed much sin against Thee and Thy dear Son Jesus Christ. Oh! I pray thee, God, to be very pitiful to me, a poor guilty sinner. Oh! my God into Thy hands I commit my soul. O God, accept me for Thine only Son's name's sake. O God, I am very thankful to Thee this morning for giving me health and sleep. Keep me from telling lies or bearing false witness against my dear poor companions this day. Oh! give them new hearts ; make them good, happy and wise, for they do not understand what Thou art. O Lord God, for the sake of Christ. Amen."

Many great men have found the manual alphabet of the deaf and dumb useful at different times. On one occasion an English judge, while on one of his circuits, lost his way to the next assize town, and none of his party knew the road. A deaf and dumb woman came upon them at two cross roads. The judge eagerly enquired of her the way to the town he was destined to hold assizes at, but she pointed to her ears and mouth and shook her head, to tell him that she was deaf and dumb, and did not understand him. The judge was in despair and turned to retrace his steps; but one of his party who had learned the alphabet of the deaf and dumb, spelled the name of the town to her, and she instantly pointed to the direction where the road led to the place. The judge gave her a shilling and rode on. He afterwards learned the alphabet himself, and soon found it useful in the trial of an unfortunate deaf-mute for robbery. He astonished all in the court by talking with the prisoner on his fingers and acting as interpreter for the lawyers.

The well-known authoress, Charlotte Elizabeth, was quite deaf, like Dr. Kitto, the author of many valuable books on the Bible and Bible lands. Her husband became very expert in the use of the finger alphabet, and used to translate to her sermons and speeches in Parliament as quickly as they were delivered by the speakers.

Some years ago in a village church in Yorkshire, there might have been seen a very intelligent young girl interpreting the sermon to her deaf and dumb parents, between whom she sat during the service.

The attention of the girl to the voice of the preacher, and the velocity with which she worked her fingers to convey to the eyes of her parents what she heard, excited great surprise in all who saw her for the first time thus employed.

The value of the deaf-mute alphabet to people not deaf and dumb has often been shown in different ways. We could write many interesting anecdotes illustrating the value of

" That wondrous bridge, no bigger than the hand,
   By which truth travels to the silent land,"

had we time and space at our disposal. One more anecdote of the alphabet, and we will turn to something else.

Some years ago, a poor, homeless deaf and dumb girl in London was taken into service by a lady, and taught house-work. Her mistress learned the alphabet to communicate with her, and soon became expert in its use. Her husband, who was a banker, also learned it, and the girl became as easily to manage as if she were not deaf and dumb. One day the husband was obliged to bring to his home the treasures of the bank on account of a fire there. This came to the knowledge of a burglar, who secreted himself in the bedroom of the lady, where the treasure was deposited. The lady retired to bed while the husband was absent on business. She soon heard sneezing under the bed, but remained quiet, as if asleep. The burglar then emerged from his hiding-place and demanded of the lady to know where the money was deposited. She was terrified at his threats and referred him to an iron safe in a corner. While he was trying to open it he heard the footsteps of the husband ascending the stairs, and he rushed to his former hiding-place, threatening the lady with instant death if she said a word about him or left the room. The husband noticed his wife's paleness and asked her what was the matter. She answered aloud, " I have a bad headache," and immediately spelled on her fingers, " Hush, there is a robber under the bed." The husband answered, " My dear, I am sorry for your headache ; you must have a cup of tea," and thrust the poker into the fire, saying it was a cold night. When the poker was red hot, he turned to the servant man who had come into the room, and said, " Thomas, there is a man under the bed. Do you think this hot poker will bring him out ? " The burglar at once left his hiding-place and begged for mercy. "How did you know I was here ? " he said. " The lady did not tell you, I know she did not speak one word about me." He was given into custody and afterwards sent over the seas to a distant penal settlement, and never knew how his presence under the bed was revealed to the gentleman. The gentleman became a very warm friend to deaf-mutes and their schools ever afterwards.

The sign language of the deaf and dumb in the hands of an experienced teacher often shows its vast importance in trying circumstances. One anecdote which came to the knowledge of the writer will suffi-ciently illustrate this:—A few years ago, the London police found a deaf and dumb woman, totally unedu-cated, wandering about the streets at midnight. She could give no account of herself, and the police kindly took her to the workhouse near by for safe keeping. Every effort of the officers of the workhouse to discover her name and residence failed. A mission-ary to the deaf and dumb was sent for to try to find out from where she had come. He found she was utterly ignorant of the alphabet, nor could she read or write. He soon found by her signs that she had been brought by railway to London by a man with whiskers and then deserted. Now, as no signs could discover her name and residence, the missionary was in a diffi-culty. He, however, did not give her case up as hope-less, but hired a cab and told the driver to drive wher-ever she might direct. She directed them on up one street and down another till they came to the London Bridge Station. The missionary asked her in signs if they were to get out. She shook her head to say " No." On they went till they came to the steamboat landing. She then told him to stop and get out. The sight of the steamboat gave her great pleasure, and the mission-ary understood by her signs that she was to go on board one of the steamers, and pointed towards Lam-beth. Tickets were bought for that place, and on arrival there the young woman was overjoyed, and jumped

out of the boat, making eager signs to her kind friend
to follow.   They then hastened on foot through several
streets, the young woman acting as guide, till they
came to a house, which she entered.   A ticket was in
the window with " This House to Let " on it, which the
missionary read with some misgiving, and presently
the young woman returned with a sad countenance,
signing to the missionary that her parents or friends
had gone away !   The missionary made enquiries of
the neighbors, and they informed him that the occup-
ants of the house had left a few days ago, and gone to
another part of London.   He obtained their names
and the address to which they had removed, and soon
found the girl's parents, who were overwhelmed with
joy at the recovery of their poor daughter, whom they
said had been decoyed away by a bad man.

Deaf-mutes sometimes make funny sentences in trying to learn the English language.   At one school a
little deaf-mute boy was asked to show his skill in the
use of the English language on his slate, and he wrote :
" A man ran from a cow.   He is a coward."   He thus
unconsciously perpetrated a pun, which caused the
visitors great amusement.

A few years ago, an English lady was teaching a
school for hearing children in Demerara ; and a colored
deaf and dumb girl came to learn to read and write.
The missionary's wife and the teacher shook their
heads, and thought that it was impossible, and signed
for her to go home.   Day by day she came to the
school and would not be refused.   At last the teacher
wrote to England for the deaf and dumb alphabet.   It
was surprising how quickly the poor girl learned the
English language.   By-and-bye she could read the
New Testament, from which she learned to love Jesus
as her Saviour.   One day she wrote to her kind teacher,
" Missie, me too happy.   You would think when me
walk out that there were two peoples in the road, but
it is *Jesus and me*.   He talk and me talk, and we two
too happy together."

A deaf and dumb pupil of the great French land-
scape painter Corot (who died in 1875), got from his
master a paper on which was written "Conscience,"
which so impressed the deaf-mute that in copying one

of his beautiful pencil drawing he even tried to imitate a stain of glue. Corot, when he saw it, smiled, and wrote to him : " Very well, my friend ; but when you are before Nature you will not see any stains."

In speaking of deaf-mute artists, I would like to tell an anecdote of the Scotch deaf-mute artist, Walter Geikie, whose interesting biography was written by the late Sir T. D. Lauder, Bart. Geikie was a very clever artist, and has left many much-prized drawings. He died in 1837. An anecdote regarding an individual who makes a very conspicuous appearance among the characters found in his etchings, is worth relating as an example of the difficulties he encountered in his ardent desire to collect the portraits of people whom he saw in the streets of Edinburgh. The porter of the Grass-market was a singular character and arrested Geikie's attention. He was somewhat pot-bellied, and with that projection and hang of the nether lip, and elevation of nose that give to the human countenance a certain air of vulgar importance. In this subject it seemed to say: "Though I'm a porter, I'm no fool." Geikie had made several attempts to get near enough to sketch this man. Day after day he hunted his intended victim with pencil and sketch-book, but failed to get a chance of him. The porter perceived him, and suspecting his intention, at once moved on and plunged into the crowd. Like a young Highland sportsman, who wishes to get a shot at an old fox who may have dodged into cover, Geikie, with pencil and paper in hand, prowled about after his prey. But the porter was on his guard and took good care to keep behind other people, so as to defy the attempts of the young artist, until at last, when the market began to thin, and his hopes of defeating the foul intention against him ebbed away with the lessening crowd, he lost all patience, and abused and threatened his tormenter with great fury, both of words and of actions. The first were of course lost upon the poor deaf lad, although there was no mistaking the meaning shake of the porter's mutton fists. But as this only threw his subject into a more tempting attitude, the artist's fervor for his art rendered him utterly regardless of consequences, and he tried his pencil with great enthusiasm !

This enraged the porter, who roared like an infuriated bull, and rushed at Geikie to punish him for his boldness; and before Geikie had time to apply his pencil to the paper, he was obliged to fly to save his bones. The porter's heavy weight prevented anything like an equal race, so Geikie kept ahead and made rapid sketches of his approaching foe at every stop he made, as they ran up the Grassmarket. The porter was all the time puffing and blowing and laboring after him, and his fury seemed to be increased at every step. He made use of every nerve to catch the young artist, which prevented him making further use of his pencil. Fortunately an open stair of one of the large buildings most opportunely presented itself, into which Geikie rushed, and the porter remained outside watching for the return of his enemy. He stood outside with his hands under the tails of his coat. Geikie had a capital view of him from one of the windows, and immediately set to work with his pencil and executed an admirable sketch of one of the most curious men of Edinburgh, who has long since passed away. When the sketch was executed Geikie found that the porter kept watch for him, so he had to remain in his hiding place for several hours. When, at last, the porter got tired of keeping sentry and moved away, Geikie emerged from his retreat, went home, and saw him no more. In the collection of this clever deaf artist the reader will find the remarkable character above described in the plate entitled "Street Auctioneer," and he is in the act of consulting his old-fashioned chronometer.

Many more interesting and amusing anecdotes could be told of deaf-mute artists (for there are many of them in England), and of deaf-mutes in various other professions, but space is limited. Sometimes deaf-mutes display great intelligence and attain to a respectable niche of fame in art, science and literature. We will mention one instance of the extraordinary intellectual calibre of a congenital deaf-mute—a prodigy. Some years ago a benevolent gentleman found a red-headed, ragged little deaf-mute in the streets of Glasgow, and took him to the school for deaf-mutes in that city. He showed considerable intelligence, and the gentleman thought he was a rough diamond but capable of being highly

polished by education and training. During the first
session at school the boy shot ahead of every other
pupil, and there were then more than a hundred, many
of them having been there for seven or eight years.
The rapidity with which he learned was amazing;
indeed his memory was so retentive that what he once
read he never forgot. Such was the calibre of his
mind that nothing was too difficult for his comprehension. He read books on mathematics, metaphysics
and the like, whether they were printed in English,
foreign or dead languages, which he also read with ease.
When school was over, he would rush to the library,
take out a lot of books under his arms, and make his
way to the nearest fire to read them, while his school-
mates directed their steps to the play-ground. Such,
was the force of habit that he would sit near the fire
even during summer while he studied. No wonder
with a mind so well stored with knowledge, he was a
capital story-teller. He never used signs since the
day he could spell on his fingers. He was appointed
an assistant-teacher at the school, but he found the task
too irksome, and left the institution to become a common
laborer in order to make money more rapidily to
purchase books. He spent all his money in books and
neglected his bodily wants. His books increased in
number very fast, and they formed his table, chair and
bed, by being piled one upon another in his lodgings.
They were his only articles of furniture. The extraordinary learning of this deaf and dumb laborer attracted the attention of many gentlemen and his employers,
who thought that he was not in his proper sphere.
They determined to give him a better position so that
his fund of knowledge might be put to some use.
They visited his lodgings for this purpose one day,
when he was not at his work, and found him dead on
his bed of books, having literally starved his body to
death to feed his hungry mind. He had everything
ready for writing a book, which he said would astonish
the world. There were several reams of paper and a
large bottle of ink, showing that he fully intended to
enter upon the work, but there was no indication of
what work it would be. His stock of books were
printed in several languages of the highest kind of
literature. He was sixteen or eighteen years old when

c

he died. He had a florid countenance, red hair, greenish eyes inclining to blue, which give him a peculiar expression.

The following is an extract from a deaf-mute's letter to his teacher in Glasgow, Dr. Anderson :

" How graceful indeed is the very idea of placing some tangible token of our gratitude in the hands of our old teacher whilst bidding him welcome to the repose which he so greatly desiderates in the evening of his arduous life! For I firmly maintain that a simple address, however pregnant with the affecting pathos of a myriad of hearts overflowing with gratitude, such as that with which Dr. Peet was presented by his old pupils last year, would not do sufficient justice to our own real sentiments nor to our benefactor's merits."

Another writes in the following strain respecting the education of deaf-mutes, which contains much truth :

" The deaf-mute on leaving school, is a changed being, quite different from what he was before he went there; he is now so intelligent that he may resort to the society of the wise and good, maintain proper conduct towards his neighbors, and even hold an intercourse with that Being to whom he owes his life, with every enjoyment that can render life easy and comfortable. Under the circumstances, the education of the deaf and dumb must be among the most extraordinary and remarkable instances of philanthrophy in modern times."

The above are specimens of British deaf-mute composition which surpass anything ever penned by the famous deaf-mutes of the past century—Massieu, Clerc and many others. Who has not read the brilliant metaphorical sayings of the impracticable Massieu, the famous pupil of Abbe Sicard ? Respecting whom Dr. Buxton, Principal of the Liverpool Institution for Deaf-mutes, says : " His best replies were short, terse, pointed, and metaphorical withal. These are all characteristics of the Abbe Sicard's style, both in his writings and in his speeches; but if they are the natural characteristics of any deaf man's diction, I have been singularly unfortunate, for I have never found it so. If there is one thing they cannot do, and rarely learn to do, and never

excel in doing, it is the use of metaphors." Yet among
Massieu's sayings are these:—"Hope is the flower of
happiness," "Indifference is the neutrality of the soul,"
"Judgment is the interior sight of the mind," "Reason
is the torch of the mind, judgment is its guide,"
"Prudence is the Minerva of the soul, and rules our
words and actions," "Envy is the intellectual viper
which gnaws the heart and envenoms it," "Jealousy
is a serpent without venom," &c.

It is now well known that the questions and answers
attributed to Massieu were committed to memory, and
formed part of the system of teaching by Abbe Sicard.
Massieu was, according to his friend and school-mate,
Clerc, extremely foolish. "His childishness and vanity,
his absurd follies and oddities of conduct, were so
extravagant as sometimes to disgust even those who
worked with him, and were taught by him. His love
of finery was as ridiculous as that of Oliver Goldsmith;
and it might have been as truly said of him, as it was
of Charles II.—

> "He never said a foolish thing,
> And never did a wise one."

It was his brilliant sayings alone which made him
famous, but they have done more harm than good.
They were delusive and led people to expect every
deaf-mute taught in the Institution to be able to utter
similiar grandiloquent sentences, and to do readily and
spontaneously what they can scarcely do at all. Even
in our own time the fame of Massieu continues to
deceive and mislead. It leads to disappointment on all
sides. Parents are disappointed, subscribers are disappointed, the public are disappointed, the reputation
and possibly the funds of the Institution suffer and the
whole blame falls upon the unfortunate teacher, because
he is not Sicard, and cannot turn out, not one Massieu,
but a score or a hundred.

When the Rev. T. H. Gallaudet went from America
to Europe, in 1815, to seek knowledge and experience
before he entered upon his work of deaf-mute instruction in the Western World, he found Massieu and Clerc
in the full vigour of their powers, and at the height of
their fame. He first visited England without finding

what he sought, and went away, disappointed, to
France. He was, in fact, compelled to decide upon his
course, and make his choice at Paris. Whom, then,
did he select as his co-worker and life companion?
Not Massieu, but Clerc. Not the repeater of sparkling
answers, but the practical, solid, working teacher. His
whole life shows that the founder of the American
Asylum was a man of great sagacity. The late Dr.
Peet, President of the New York Institution, in the
published report of his visit to the various schools for
the deaf and dumb in Europe, in 1841, says, respecting
Massieu—"Even Massieu, whose fame a few brilliant
answers given at public exercises have spread through
the world, was after testimony of those who knew him
best, unable to write a page in correct French, or to follow out to any length a consecutive chain of reasoning."
Then after citing Clerc, by way of contrast, and as
showing what a pupil of rare talent may become, in
spite of the defects of the system under which he was
trained, Dr. Peet finishes the paragraph by saying,
"Such is the prevalent judgment passed upon Sicard
in Paris; I only repeat it." (Report on European
Institutions, page 98.)

In speaking of the disappointment caused by the
brilliant answers of Massieu, an anecdote recorded in
Dr. Orpen's work, " Anecdotes of the Deaf and Dumb,"
may here be introduced and read by every one with
profit, as it shows the absurd expectations as to the
progress of deaf-mute children entertained by persons
who forget the excessive difficulty of their instruction.
Rev. J. D. Hastings, speaking at the tenth annual meeting of the Deaf and Dumb Institution, Dublin, said:
" I wish to mention one fact which came under my
notice. I happened to be at the Institution on a visit-
ing day ; there were several persons present at the
time ; among the number was a lady and her son, with
whom I have the honour to be acquainted; the lady
is now within the hearing of my voice; she asked
one of the little girls, I believe, the smallest in the
school (Cecilia White), a question ; she had it written
on the slate; it was, 'Do you remember the first promise of the Messiah ?' The children looked and looked
again, and then made a sign to know what was Messiah;

the lady wrote on the slate, 'the Anointed or Sent.' The little girl looked again, then looked at me, and made a sign, by pointing to her head, to say she did not know. The lady turned to me and said, 'Now I am convinced the Bible is not taught in the school; I was informed before of this, but I determined on judging for myself.' I endeavored to show her that it was quite unreasonable to expect a child, who was deaf and dumb, to have that knowledge which other children possess. I found all was in vain. I then said to her, 'Perhaps you would permit me to ask your son (who to all appearance was three or four years older than the little girl), a similar question.' The lady at once assented. I asked him could he tell me, 'What was the second promise of the Messiah?' After some time I looked for an answer; but no, the boy was as dumb as the little girl. His mamma looked at him, but no answer. At length I said, 'Perhaps the question is too difficult; but I will be satisfied if you remove the odium from the dumb girl, and consquently from the Institution; tell me, What was the first promise of the Messiah?' No answer, he could not tell. In vain the mamma looked with anxious eye; but alas! no reply. The lady said, 'Answer the question, my dear,' 'Indeed,' mamma,' said he, 'I cannot.' Thus was the Institution brought into disgrace; while a boy three or four years older and possessed of those faculties which had been denied to this poor girl, was unable to answer the question. I thanked the little boy, and said, 'I would not say that he did not read his Bible, nor would I say to the lady that it was not taught in her family; but I would say the question was beyond his comprehension. After some further examination of the little girl, the lady was quite satisfied that the Bible was taught in the school; and I am happy to say, sir, that we have not only that lady's guinea, but her good wishes, with a determination to forward the views of the Institution so far as she possibly can."

QUEEN VICTORIA regrets that she cannot use the deaf and dumb alphabet now so fast as when she was young. Her Majesty learned the signs in order to converse with the deaf-mute daughter of a cottager near Osborne, Isle of Wight, several years ago.—*Montreal Witness,* 10th Dec., 1879.

CHAPTER V.

The Systems of Instruction.

THERE are three systems employed in teaching deaf-mutes, viz:

The *Mechanical Articulation Method*, which is the oldest of all systems, was invented by Heinicke, a Saxon, about the year 1750. This system aims at developing the powers of speech, and the educating of the eye of the pupil to perform as far as it can the part of the ear. This system is now greatly assisted by Visible Speech, invented by Professor A. Melville Bell, late of London, England, and now of Brantford, Ontario. It is now employed in most institutions for deaf-mutes. For semi-mutes, or those who have learned to speak before becoming deaf, this method is the best.

The *Natural Method*, or the language of pantomime. This system was founded by Abbe L'Epee of Paris, and is employed chiefly in the United States and France. By this method signs are used at every stage of the pupils' instruction, and is often carried to excess in many schools, preventing the pupils from acquiring a good command of their native language. For imparting religious instruction, lecturing and communicating with uneducated deaf-mutes this method is exceedingly convenient.

The *Combined Method* is a system of instruction embracing the first and second methods which, we believe, was first used by Thomas Braidwood in London. In schools employing this system the teachers recognize the utility of the sign-language, and use articulation where practicable. This system enables the teacher to teach deaf-mutes of all degrees of intellect and none are turned away without deriving more or less benefit from it. It calls to the aid of the teacher every new or old plan which may have been found to be benefical or of value in imparting instruction to either the congenital deaf-mute or the semi-mute. The *combined method* is employed in all the large Institutions in Europe and America, and is growing more and more popular every year.

CHAPTER VI.

The Mental and Moral Condition of the Uneducated Deaf-mutes.—No Ideas of a Creator.—Is Conscience Primitive?

WE have frequently been asked for information respecting the deaf-mute's ideas of God and the soul previous to his instruction. This subject has often been discussed by learned men. The testimonies of deaf-mutes themselves are substantially alike, as to their having had no idea of the Creator before instruction.

To the twenty-second report of the American Asylum are annexed several questions, addressed to a number of pupils, whose average age on joining the school was about fourteen. "Before you were instructed in the Asylum had you any idea of the Creator?" The answers, substantially alike, are given by thirteen pupils. "No, I did not know that a Creator existed. I had no idea of God at all before I entered the Asylum." "Had you reasoned or thought about the world, or the beings and things it contains?" "I never attempted to suppose who had made the world, or how it had ever come into existence." "Had you any idea of your own soul?" "I never conceived such a thing as a soul, nor was I ever conscious that my mind had faculties and operations different and distinct from those of my body." Their answers show how little their friends at home had been able to teach them.

The mental and moral condition of the uneducated deaf-mute has been found to be so low that men of science and education have asked "Is conscience primitive?"

It was only recently that our attention was called to an article on this subject in the *Popular Science Monthly* by the editor of the *Canadian Illustrated News,* who requested our views on the matter. There seems to be much ground for the belief that conscience is not primitive in the *congenital deaf-mute* before instruction. We have, after nearly twenty years' experience as a teacher of deaf-mutes and from personal experience, been led to believe that "conscience" as now understood—the internal self-knowledge or judgment of right and wrong, the knowledge of our own actions as well as those of others—is an *acquired faculty* in the deaf-mute. We possess no record of a congenital deaf-mute who, by his own unaided efforts, has found the being of a God, or discovered the fact of his own immortality. His mind is indeed dark and inert—in fact, hermetically sealed. How could it be otherwise in his condition? Locke says that man has no innate ideas, but that his mind in early infancy is like a *blank* sheet of paper, ready to receive any external impressions. So with the uneducated deaf-mute. His mind remains a blank as long as he is uninstructed. The famous Abbe Sicard, of Paris, a world-renowned teacher of deaf-mutes, says that "a deaf-mute (congenital and uninstructed) is a perfect cipher, a living automaton. He possesses not the sure instinct by which the animal creation is guided. He is alone in nature, with no possible exercise of his intellectual faculties which remain without action." Sicard, however, refers to the deaf-mutes of his day, nearly a hundred years ago, when through neglect, and being hidden away from society as a family disgrace, the germs of the rational and moral faculties were scarcely manifested. Such treatment of deaf-mutes in our own time is rare, and, with kindness and sympathy from the beginning, their minds have received considerable development. If conscience means internal self-knowledge, or judgment of right and wrong, a mind so dark, so inert, and wholly uninstructed as that of the uneducated congenital deaf-mute, could not reasonably be expected to possess anything like it. Uneducated deaf-mutes seldom exhibit compunctions of conscience when they have done anything wrong, but such symptoms gradually appear as they grow older and some instruction is imparted. The testimony of educated deaf-mutes themselves goes to support this view, and the personal experience and observation of the writer confirms it to a great extent.

Their moral and intellectual condition before instruction is little *above* that of the more intelligent brutes, and *lower* than that of the most unenlightened savages. All philologists and mental philosophers agree that it is the gift of language that chiefly distinguishes man from the brutes, and that without it he would have little claim to the title of a rational being. The testimony of educated deaf-mutes throws much light upon the amount of knowledge they possessed before coming under systematic instruction. Very few of them had any idea of the creation of the world, or of the plants and animals which it contains. Their own reflections, and all the imperfect attempts of their friends to instruct them, have failed to give them any idea of the existence of a God or the soul. We need not wonder at this when we read that Ovid, who lived in the learned and polished era of Augustus, expressed the popular belief of his time in the theory that all things were produced by the due union of heat and moisture, which shows that deaf-mutes have not been alone in the utter ignorance of the existence of a Creator. The existence of the soul after death has never occurred to the uneducated mute. All the efforts of anxious parents to convey some idea to this end have failed. The pointing to the fire to convey an idea of hell impresses the mute that the body will be thrown into a fire for some cause by some person at some indefinite time. Before receiving instruction the writer, whose home was within sight of the parish church and the county jail, had his notions of heaven and hell formed by his mother always pointing to one or to the other of those buildings according to the nature of his conduct or actions. If he required reproof she would point to the jail and fire, but if she wished to show that she was pleased with his behaviour she would pat his head and point to the church, and then upwards and assume a reverent look. From this mode of control he formed his idea that the church was the place for those who had fine clothes and were well behaved, and that the minister was the object of worship or admiration. The jail he thought was for the poor, the drunkard, and those that robbed orchards, who were there cast bodily into a fire. Having observed a man in the street whom he once saw taken into a jail, his astonishment was very great on finding that neither the man's person nor his clothes had been burned. The next time his mother threatened him with the terrors of the jail and the fire for misconduct, he gazed at her with a look of incredulity, shook his head and laughed. Queer ideas about death have been

D

entertained by uneducated deaf-mutes. Most of them
have thought that death was only sleep, and to put a
body in a coffin and bury it seemed to them to be an
act of cruelty. They have no sense of moral wrong-
doing. They think they ought to be allowed to do just
as they please, no matter what it may be. A most
intelligent lady, a congenital mute, who had reached a
nature age before receiving any systematic instruction,
confessed that she had been practicing falsehood for
many years without the slightest notion that she was
doing wrong. This is not an uncommon fault with
this class of people. Another of great intelligence had
been in the habit of falsehood and dishonesty without
any compunctions of conscience. He never dreamed
that he was doing wrong, and only dreaded the punish-
ment which followed detection. Many instances could
be cited if necessary from deaf-mute testimony in
support of the assertion that the *uneducated* deaf-mute
has no moral sense of right and wrong. He is a practical
atheist, and if his friends have tried to give him an idea
of a Supreme Power and such takes root in his mind,
his conceptions on the point are most vague and unsatisfactory. Teachers of deaf-mutes have frequently
watched the gradual development of the mind of their
new pupils. It is found that, by associating among the
other pupils, the new arrivals will soon gain the idea of
a Being existing above "who can see them, and is
angry when they behave badly," and the pointing
upwards is often used by one pupil as a check upon
another who is inclined to be naughty. Sometimes it
has this effect, but we have more than once seen the
admonitions defied by young deaf-mutes who had not
yet obtained clear ideas on the subject. We have seen
them disputing and their antagonistic principles
aroused when one has been desirous of saying something especially annoying to his opponent, who, he
knows, has a reverence for the Being above, and is
shocked when anything is said against Him. He will
say in his signs "God-bad," not knowing his blasphemy,
yet with a secret shrug that he has gained his point,
beaten his antagonist, who rushes with horror expressed on his countenance to report to his teacher the
profanity of the other.

When the deaf-mute is put under careful control he comes to associate in his mind a line of conduct with what produces pain, and another line of conduct with what produces pleasure. Out of this grows a *sort of conscience* which leads him to be sorrowful when he does certain things, and to be glad when he does the contrary. This conscience is entirely dependent upon the person to whom he is subjected. "Given a good master," says Dr. Peet, the highest authority in America, "and he will be very likely to have a kind of moral sense that will be a safe guide in the life he leads, and will bring about habits that will be useful to him hereafter." So quite the reverse will be his conduct if he be placed under a bad master. He may be obedient, diligent, affectionate, habitually honest, but it will be owing to the influence of kind and firm control and good example—*not* to the higher moral and religious motives that are addressed to children who hear. He is too often self-willed, passionate, prone to secret vices and suspicious, but these bad qualities are generally the outcome of parental indulgence, and in having been the butt ·of thoughtless young people.

Is the uneducated deaf-mute morally and legally responsible? is a question which has been often discussed. In many criminal cases, both in Europe and America, uneducated deaf-mutes have frequently figured for murder, but they have been treated as irresponsible beings, and no sentence has been passed on them.

There can be no more pitiable object than an uneducated deaf-mute, except where blindness is added to that of deafness. His condition points to conclusions which cannot be evaded. It is the duty of society to provide for his instruction at the proper age, and it is criminal on the part of parents and guardians who neglect to secure for their unfortunate child the benefits within their reach. To the deaf-mute education means *everything*. It means intercourse with fellow-men, hope, happiness,. the pleasant communion with the highest intellectual achievements of men of all countries and all ages, which we find in books. It makes life in this world enjoyable and gives him hope

of salvation in the world to come. To deny the deaf-
mute education is to keep his mind on a level with the
brutes. " To the hearing child," says Dr. Peet, " every
word spoken in his presence is a means of intellectual
development. Every person, literate or illiterate, with
whom he comes in contact is for the time his conscious
or unconscious teacher. In fact school gives him so
small a portion of the knowledge he possesses that it
may be considered rather the regulator than the source
of his attainments. To the deaf-mute it means home,
happiness; it means the full and free exercise of all
the rights, immunities and privileges which belong
to humanity."

CHAPTER VII.

Marriages Among Deaf-mutes.

WE will now considered *the marriage of the deaf
and dumb with each other.* We have known people
to declare that such unions are very wicked, and ought
not to be allowed ; but their opinion is mainly founded
on the belief that this intermarriage invariably perpe-
tuates the infirmity, which is quite a mistake. We
admit that the children of deaf and dumb parents are
occasionally similarly afflicted, but the cases are rare—
they are quite the exception. In London we know of
114 instances of this kind of union ; 76 marriages have
had offspring, but in only seven of these instances is
the offspring deaf and dumb, and in these cases one
or more of the brothers or sisters of one of the parents
have been so afflicted. On the other hand, we know
of deaf and dumb parents who have had as many as
nine children, not one of which was deaf; we
have known, on the contrary, cases where both parents
have had all their faculties, but out of ten children
five have been deaf and dumb; and the report of the
London Asylum gives an instance where out of ten
children eight were deaf and dumb. This argument,
therefore, of perpetuating deafness, though it may
be thus applied in the least degree, is not, says
the Rev. S. Smith, chaplain of the Royal Association
for the Deaf and Dumb, London, strong enough
to support any one in prohibiting such marriages

as wicked, when other facts are taken into consideration; for since it is shown that it is in quite
exceptional cases that the offspring of these intermarriages inherit the same infirmity, it will not be denied
that deaf-mutes have a right to marry as well as other
persons, and whom they ought to marry depends upon
each one's choice and acceptance. Now it will readily
be granted that there will be the most sympathy and
love between persons whose feelings, tastes, and habits
offer a certain resemblance, and who can communicate
freely with each other. Comparatively *few* hearing
people know the deaf and dumb language, and a very
small proportion of those who do would marry a deaf
and dumb person, unless some advantage were connected with the union : indeed it may be that in the
whole of a deaf and dumb man's hearing acquaintances
not one eligible female knows his language ; it is evident therefore that he will generally seek a wife amongst
those of his own class, and in London, the instances
existing and known to us where this intermarriage
has taken place stand in the proportion of *four* to *one*
where the woman can hear. Again, not many hearing
men would marry a deaf and dumb woman without a
consideration as a "make-weight." Only four cases of
this kind are known to us in London. Besides, we
have been told by very respectable deaf and dumb
females that they would not marry a man who could
hear; they would not have confidence in him ; he
would not take the trouble to tell them *everything* ;
perhaps he would have hearing friends come to see
him, and then they would be shut out from the general
conversation; they would prefer one like themselves—
one who had no advantages over them. We argue,
nevertheless, that the best wife for a deaf and dumb
man—if he can find one and persuade her to marry
him—is a woman who *can hear*, one who has acquired
a ready means of communication with him, sympathizes
with his affliction, and so is prepared to take upon herself a larger share than ordinary of the management of
their family and joint affairs, which must devolve upon
her on account of her husband's deprivation; and the
higher and best educated class, as a rule, do obtain
this kind of wife ; their eyes are open to the advantages
of such a help-meet. As one of them has written :

" When a man marries, he ought to try and supply
that wherein he is deficient; a deaf and dumb man
wants some one to hear and speak for him.... A deaf
man taking a deaf woman to be his companion would
find the various hindrances which he meets in his
daily life doubled and increased; he would be obliged
to go to some one else than his wife to interpret or to
explain for him." The hearing sisters or daughters of
deaf and dumb persons would be most likely to fulfil
the necessary requirements; and it so happens that the
hearing wife of one deaf-mute gentleman, who is much
praised by her husband, had a brother similarly afflicted, of whom she was very fond; but death snatching
him away from her love, she took the opportunity of
supplying his place by a husband from the same class,
and an excellent wife she has proved. We also know
other similar cases with the same happy result. But,
returning to the general rule prevalent amongst them
of intermarriage amongst themselves, we can bear
testimony that when two are well-matched, intelligent,
and of amiable disposition, and especially if they act
from Christian principle, they get on together exceedingly well. There is, however, some disadvantage as
regards their children; they cannot receive early instruction in spoken language and moral training: they
may learn vulgar expressions from other children, and
use them towards each other in their parents' presence
without their cognizance, and in this they are unable
to correct them. Some of these disadvantages are,
however, soon overcome by an early attendance at
school. The children of the deaf and dumb soon learn
to communicate with their parents by signs, and it is
very amusing to see little things two or three years
old beginning thus to make known their wants to
them. So that, taking all these circumstances into
consideration, we may consistently state that deaf-mute
intermarriages are not advisable in those cases where a
suitable hearing partner can be obtained, but they are
not wicked, nor are they to be prohibited, lest a worse
thing come to pass. Still this precaution should be
taken by the deaf and dumb, not to choose those in
whose families any hereditary tendency has manifested
itself.

In Canada and the United States there are many deaf-mute unions. Perhaps no country in the world shows so many deaf-mute intermarriages as does the latter country, and many of them have produced deaf-mute children, but it has not been found necessary to prohibit or discourage them on that account. There are about a dozen deaf-mute married couples in the Dominion of Canada, and most of them have families, but none, as far as we have been able to learn, have deaf-mute children.

CHAPTER VIII.

Blind Deaf-mutes.—Laura Bridgman.—Mary Bradley.—Joseph Hague.—Anecdotes —Death of Hague. —Other Cases on Record.

THERE are, happily, but few human beings who in addition to the loss of hearing are also deprived of sight, and are therefore at once deaf, dumb, and blind. These appear to be so entirely cut off from the outer world that the position seems at first sight beyond the reach of amelioration; and was until a comparatively recent date believed to be so, even by those whose ingenuity was daily taxed to find means to reach the minds of those who are deprived of hearing only.

The case of a deaf, dumb, and blind youth, the son of a Scotch minister, attracted a large amount of attention early in the last century. Curiosity was excited to watch the habits of the youth, in order to see whether there was not some loophole by which light might be made to penetrate the darkness within, but nothing could be devised which yielded any result.

It was not until the wonderful revelation of the case of Laura Bridgman by the late Charles Dickens was made in his "American Notes" in 1842-3, that attention was again awakened to the consideration of blind deaf-mutes, and the possibility of reaching and developing a mind so completely isolated. The statements made by Mr. Dickens were of so extraordinary a character that few persons—especially those engaged in educating the deaf and dumb—could give them credence, and many persons concluded that he must have been imposed upon, or that the narrative was only " the tale of a traveller," related to astonish and amuse.

About the time when "American Notes" appeared, a member of the Committee of the Institution reported a case of complete blindness and deafness, in a child named Mary Bradley, which had come under his observation at the infant department of the Parochial Schools of the Manchester Union. This excited the curiosity and kind interest of the head master, Mr. Andrew Patterson, and it was proposed he and the member of the Committee should examine the case and see if there were any possibility of doing anything with it.

From all that could be ascertained about the child, it appears she was then about seven years old, and that she had lost her sight and hearing about three years previously, having been abandoned by her mother in a damp cellar while suffering from some virulent disease. The mother, it was understood, was a loose woman, who had left her husband and subsequently her child, and had taken to evil courses. It was believed, at the time the child was received into the Institution for the Deaf and Dumb, that both parents were dead.

Having succeeded in getting the child placed in his charge, Mr. Patterson had next to decide upon some mode of proceeding with her, and the obvious course seemed to be to watch her habits, and to endeavour to adapt his own course and the efforts of those around her to them. With this view she was left for some days to her own resources, in order that the bent of her inclination might be seen and judged of. Finding herself in a new position, she was occupied for a time in becoming acquainted with the locality, and the persons and things by which she was surrounded. She made no attempt to make known her wants by signs, as is usual in the case of the deaf and dumb. If she required help her habit was to shout and scream, and as her utterances were by no means agreeable, every one was interested in relieving her wants. Since her loss of hearing and sight she had been in no position in which signs could have been understood, had she made any, but it never seemed to occur to her to do so. In fact, she was at the time one of the most uncouth and wild-looking objects it is well possible to conceive. She had recently had her head shaved in consequence of some disease in the skin of the scalp, and with a crouching, groping attitude, she had more the appearance of a scared and timid animal seeking some mode of esacpe from danger or unpleasant position, than of a human being endowned with a rational soul.

The first step in teaching seemed to be to make her acquainted with the names of the objects around her. With this view, then, Mr. Patterson selected those objects which differed materially in form from each other, viz., a *pen*, a *book*, and a *slate* As the visible letters could not be submitted to her, the signs used by the deaf and dumb were given on the fingers instead, Mr. Patterson giving the signs by touching her fingers with his, in the proper form. Thus the *pen* was placed in her hands; she felt its firm, elastic quality, etc.; then the letters *p e n* were signed on her fingers, and an endeavour made to indicate to her that the signs meant the object which she had been handling. The other words *book* and *slate* were indicated in the same way; but she failed to understand the connection between these arbitrary signs and the things handled. It never seemed to occur to her that the signs had any reference to the objects.

In the case of children who can hear or see, the, sounds of the letters or the forms of the signs are at once a key to their application to the object named, but in this case there was no clue to the meaning, as at present they had neither sound nor form to her mind. An hour or two, day after day, was devoted to the accomplishment of this first and all-important step; but the labour seemed entirely without effect. No progress towards success was made, and every day the work had to be commenced anew, and unfortunately was followed by the same results as on the previous days, without any progress. Every means were tried to arrive at some degree of success. The appliances were varied as much as possible, but still apparently without any intelligence on the part of the pupil. Her kind and assiduous teacher could only devote to her the hours in which he could be spared from the routine work of a large school. He continued these attempts for four or five weeks, and almost in despair of any good results began to think of abandoning his efforts,

E

at least for a period; when all at once, like a sudden
burst of sunshine, her countenance brightened up one
day with a full intelligence beaming in it. She had
found the key to the mystery! Placing her hand on
each of the objects separately, she gave the name of
each on her fingers, or rather signed them on the
fingers of her teacher as her mode of describing them.

Thus the first step was attained at last, and the chief
difficulty cleared away for overcoming the next. It
was a comparatively easy matter now to proceed and
enlarge the vocabulary of the names of the objects
most familiar to her. Mr. Patterson then cut out the
letters of the alphabet in cardboard, and gummed them
to a sheet of stiff pasteboard, so that they stood in
relief, and could be sharply felt and distinguished from
each other by the fingers. By this means she soon
became acquainted with all their forms, and mentally
associated—say *p e n*—with the signs upon her fingers
and the object which these signs represented. Her
progress now became daily more and more evident.
She took great delight in her work, and with the
limited time at Mr. Patterson's disposal, it was difficult
to keep pace with her desire for the knowledge of
names. From these she was taught the quality of
things. When new words of this kind were intended
to be taught, the objects were generally placed before
her, as an illustration of comparison; for instance—a
large book and a small one, a light object and a heavy
one, thick and thin, rough and smooth, hard and soft,
sweet and sour. Objects possessing opposite qualities
were placed within her reach, and she very readily
acquired the words to express them. Thus the work
went on step by step, every day's lesson being a
preparatory one for the next day. Verbs were taught
much in the same way, the word being given with the
action: standing, sitting, walking; eating, drinking,
laughing, crying, &c., generally in the form of the
present participle, and in connection with a noun,
as being an easy change from the adjectives—as, a boy
standing, a girl crying, &c.

At length the great inconvenience presented itself
of the want of a lesson-book adapted to meet the case.
In order to supply this want, a case of type for print-

ing in relief was obtained, and some lessons were printed, which were readily deciphered by the pupil through the sense of touch. It was, however, soon discovered that the operation of composing the type was an exercise which was not only very amusing to her, but also very instructive. A little box was constructed in which she could arrange the type in sentences, &c., which were dictated to her by natural signs, the teacher using her hands in the same way as he would use his own to sign similar sentences to a seeing deaf child, and this became a never-failing source of interest. It made her familiar with the various modes of construction,—the greatest difficulty which the deaf and dumb have to encounter. Every new word was at once applied to its appropriate meaning.

The effect of the dawning of this new world of intellectual life upon the temper and disposition of Mary Bradley was, at this point of her education, very unmistakable. She had hitherto been of a fretful, impatient, and very irritable temper, crying and screaming without any apparent cause; but as she made progress in her studies, this irritability gradually softened down, and she became daily more and more subdued in disposition and manner. Still at intervals, more or less prolonged, she would have fits of fretfulness and passion, which would end in a few hours in tears, when she would again resume her quiet and placid manner. These occasional outbursts would appear to have been a necessity with her. They seemed like an accumulation of humours which would burst out and expend themselves, and thus give relief for a time. Mr. Patterson and the kind friends around her soon discovered that during these paroxysms, the best and simplest course was to leave her to herself

The time occupied in teaching her to write was enormous as compared with that expended on children possessing their proper faculties. It was a work of incessant and interminable repetition; but Mr. Patterson had resolved that it must be done, and it was done accordingly.

Having once learned to write, she was enabled to correspond with friends at a distance, and to interchange letters with her sister in deprivation across the Atlantic, Laura Bridgman, who was kind enough to send her a tablet, such as she herself used. Now it must be distinctly understood that the results thus happily arrived at were attained under circumstances very different to those in which the education of Laura Bridgman was carried on—not to mention the great difference between the condition of Mary Bradley when she was rescued from the degrading and cruel associations of a pauper school, and the domestic surroundings in which Laura Bridgman had been brought up in a bright and loving home, under the care of a tender mother. From this home she was transferred to the charge of Dr. Howe, and by him placed under the special care of the lady teacher whose sole duty and pleasure it was to see to her every want, and act as her instructress. Mary Bradley, on the contrary, could only receive continuous attention for any length of time from Mr. Patterson when the duties of a large establishment permitted: and then he could only devote, what would otherwise have been his leisure, to her instruction.

At the period when Mary Bradley had been under instruction some four or five years an application was made to the Institution for the admission of a little boy suffering under the same sad privation.

Joseph Hague was the son of a deaf and dumb mother who had been educated in the Institution. He was born deaf, and became blind before he was two years old. At the period of his reception in the School for the Deaf and Dumb he was eight years old, and at once became the fellow-pupil of Mary Bradley.

On his admission he was allowed a few days to make himself familiar with the new position in which he was placed. It was very amusing to watch his explorations and to see the ready intelligence with which he made his observation.

Joseph Hague showed a considerable amount of determination and combativeness when he met with opposition. On one occasion he was walking up the school-room, in which there are two or three iron pillars to support the floor above, and forgetting that

such was the case he struck his forehead against one
of them and recoiled from it. He rubbed his forehead
for an instant, and then walked deliberately up to
the pillar and kicked it violently.

This boy, being born deaf and dumb and having
been under the care of his mother, herself a deaf-mute,
was thoroughly acquainted with the signs used by deaf
children of his age, and consequently the first steps in
the course of his instruction were easily overcome.
The progress made by the two far outstripped any
anticipations which could have been formed on the
subject from what had been previously effected by Mr.
Patterson's attention to Mary Bradley only. The
knowledge of things, gradually led on to those of a
more abstract character, and enabled their kind teacher
to show the relation between cause and effect, and by
means of things of a lower nature to reach the higher.
A knowledge of Scripture History and of God's care
for His chosen people was imparted.

During the progress of these children in their
instruction, many points peculiar to themselves and to
their condition could not fail to manifest themselves.
One peculiarity, which is perhaps more striking than
any other, was the appearance of a perception which
seemed like a new sense. The quickness of appre-
hension and understanding of what was passing around
them seemed so complete and so accurate, that it was
impossible to conceive how the mind grasped the
information unless such was the case. The boy was of
rather a mischievous disposition, and was fond of amusing himself by teasing and annoying his companion;
but it is a singular fact that the moment Mr. Patterson
entered the room he became conscious of the fact, and
instantly ceased his amusement. No doubt he had
become accustomed to the vibration caused by the
opening and shutting of the door, and by the step of
his teacher, for he could distinguish the latter from
that of every one else; and would frequently stop Mr.
P. in the room to ask a question. In addition to this,
however, both these children would receive impressions
when the sense of feeling could not be acted upon, and
they would be aware of facts which could not reach the
mind by any of the known senses. For instance, they

would sit together and hold long conversations upon each other's fingers, and while doing so Mr. Patterson would approach them with the greatest caution, and in a manner which could produce no vibration, either from his step or the movement of his body, yet they became immediately conscious of his presence, ceased their conversation, and one would inform the other that Mr. Patterson was behind them. This occurred over and over again in order to test their intelligence; every precaution and means being taken to approach without their knowledge, but always with the same results. It was quite impossible to discover by what mode they discovered the fact of the presence of their instructor; all that could be ascertained was that they *did* discover it at once.

As a further illustration of mental peculiarity it may be stated that they had an instinctive perception of character. When strangers approached them they at once put out their hands to touch them, and having done so, would either feel attracted to them or repulsed by them. In the former case they would soon put themslves on the most familiar terms with them; in the latter they would hold themselves aloof. It was the same among their school-fellows. With some, the boy especially, was on the most familiar terms, and could take any liberty with them, making them the slaves of his will; while with others he held little or no intercourse, and never voluntarily associated with them.

The sense of touch in these two children was exceedingly acute. Every person in the Institution for the Deaf and Dumb was known and recognised by them by the touch, and though many schemes were adopted occasionally to puzzle them, yet they always discovered it and named the right person. On one occasion the late Bishop of Manchester, Dr. Prince Lee, having brought some friends to visit the Institution, wished to test the boy's ability to find any one of his companions who might be named. He did so without a single failure, though they were all mixed together, and not in their usual places in the school. The boys were then made to exchange clothes, and one of them presented himself to be named. Hague at once named the boy who belonged to the clothes. On being told that he was wrong, he proceeded to manipulate the hands and features, and without hesitation gave the right name. After failing in the first instance his suspicions, were awakened, and he could not be deceived a second time.

One would imagine that persons so shut out from the influences that are apt to excite and stimulate vanity in dress, would be quite free from any weakness of this kind; but it is not so. Mary Bradley was quite a connoisseur in dress, and was fond of feeling the dresses and trimmings of those within her reach, and giving her opinion. On one occasion two ladies, dressed in every respect alike, both as to pattern and material, came under her manipulation. She said, or rather signed, that they were very nice, but that one dress was much better than the other. The ladies said she was mistaken, as they were exactly alike, being made of the same material, cut from the same piece of fabric. She, however, insisted that they were not alike, and that one dress was much better than the other. No difference could be detected by any one else; but Mary Bradley was found to be right. From subsequent inquiry it was discovered that the person from whom the material was bought had not sufficient of the one piece for two dresses, and had opened another piece, supplied by the same manufacturer, from which he cut sufficient for one of the dresses, believing it to be in every respect the exact quality of the other. From the delicacy of the touch of this deaf, dumb, and blind girl, the fact was detected that one piece was of superior quality to the other.

Having acquired a tolerable facility in basket-making, and becoming impatient under the restraints of the Institution, Hague became desirous of leaving. Both his parents were living, and could understand him and converse with him : it was therefore thought advisable that he should quit the school and the surveillance of his worthy and kind teacher, Mr. Patterson, who had providentially been enabled to do so much for him ; and be placed under the supervision of his father and mother.

Mary Bradley, without a relative known to any one connected with the Institution, remained in it and

regarded it as her permanent home. Indeed, she was
generally considered as an indispensable part of it !
Her conscious life had been, as it were, awakened
within its walls and developed in its school room.
She scarcely knew of any world beyond—at least, not
in this life. During the last seven or eight years of
her earthly existence she suffered much from abscesses,
which formed in various parts of her body. She
gradually wasted away and died June, 1866, in her 26th
year, firmly believing in a future life of happiness
through Christ, leaving her bodily privations and
afflictions behind her. Nothing can be clearer than
the fact that the problem of the education of the deaf,
dumb and blind was as fully solved in her case as in
those of the more widely and popularly known
instances of Laura Bridgman and Oliver Caswell, at
the Massachusetts Institution.

Joseph Hague died in the Sheffied workhouse on the
28th February, 1879. His parents had removed there
on his leaving school at Manchester. At that time
the writer was employed at Sheffield to organize the
Association for Adult Deaf-mutes, having for its object
their religious and secular instruction. Joseph Hague
attended these services regularly and took great
delight in them. This continued until 1869, when
circumstances arose which became necessary to remove
him to the workhouse, where he was placed under the
special care of an assistant. He was a good basket-
maker, and partly supported himself after leaving
school. He continued to work at that trade while in
Union, where special privileges were allowed him by
the guardians. His greatest pleasure was to be allowed
to attend the Sabbath services, his deaf-mute friends
taking a delight in conveying instruction to him upon
his fingers, and in other ways administering to his
wants, including taking him to their homes ; and even
the poorest ungrudgingly shared their frugal meal
with him. A great portion of his time whilst in the
Workhouse was occupied in reading and committing
to memory portions of Scripture, and repeating upon
his fingers the portions so learnt, and in this manner
he had acquired a store of Scripture knowledge that
would put to shame many of his more favoured fellow-

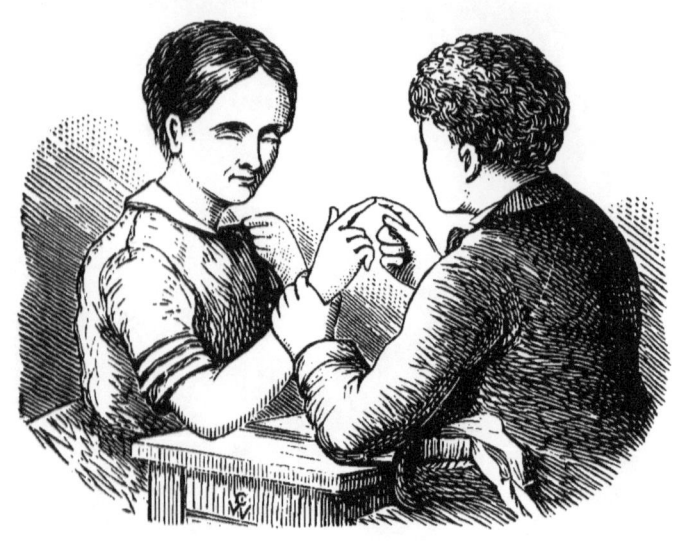

MARY BRADLEY AND JOSEPH HAGUE,
The Blind Deaf-Mutes.

creatures. On these occasions he would have a number
of words committed to memory of which he did not
know the meaning, and would most anxiously seek an
explanation of them. It was also his delight to read
the biography of great and good men, which books he
obtained from the lending library for the blind;
and it is a most remarkable fact he rarely forgot
any portion of such works, and was very conscientious
in all his dealings.

JOSEPH HAGUE.
Departed this Life on the 28th February, 1879.

Wall'd in by Deafness, Dumbness, Blindness, all!
Could Life exist beneath that dreadful pall?
It did. Life, Love were there: The living Soul
Beat hot against the bars that held it in,
Striving among the best, to reach the goal,
And, through Christ's Death, immortal Life to win.

With such a chain he laboured, on his way:
From such a chain the Soul has burst away:
The heart which throbb'd with love, hope and fear;
The Mind which strove within that dungeon drear:
The Eyes which longed in vain for earthly light,
See face to face, in God's most holy sight,
Kind Death hath bid the captive soul go free,
Where the Deaf hear, Dumb sing, and Sightless see.*

D. B.

It is very fortunate that the number of blind deaf-
mutes in the world is very small. There are nearly a
million blind people in the world and over 800,000
deaf-mutes, but the number of blind deaf-mutes
probably does not exceed 50. Of the very few who
are on record, the following may be mentioned:

1. James Mitchell, born 1795, near Inverness,
Scotland. Uneducated.

2. Hannah Lamb, London, 1808, accidentally burned
to death. Uneducated.

3. Laura Bridgman, born at Hanover, N. H., 21st
Dec., 1829. Educated by Dr. Howe, still living (1879.)

4. Oliver Caswell, South Boston. Educated at same
place as Bridgman. 1841.

* Isaiah xxxv, 5, 6.

F

5. Lucy Reed, South Boston, only partly educated.

6. Mary Bradley, born at Manchester and educated there, 1845. Was a correspondent of Laura Bridgman.

7. Joseph Hague, the school-mate of Mary Bradley, also born at Manchester. Died 28th February, 1879, at Sheffield.

8. Catherine St. Just Teskey, born in 1848 in Lower Canada, partly educated at the Protestant Institution for Deaf-mutes at Montreal in 1871,

9. James H. Coton, pupil in the New York Institution for Deaf-mutes, 1878.

10. Richard S. Clinton, pupil in the New York Institution for Deaf-mutes, 1878.

Sweden is reported to to have 20 blind deaf-mutes, an enormous number for any country in Europe. In the New York Institution there is a curious case of a boy deaf and dumb and *without arms*, who is being successfully instructed by Dr. Peet, who has taught him to write with a long pencil attached to the stumps of his arms.

CHAPTER IX.

The Comparative Happiness of the Deaf and the Blind.

A brief contrast with the blind will show the difference of the effects of the two afflictions. Speaking generally, blindness is an affliction which operates most disadvantageously upon the physical part of man; but deafness, on the contrary, affects the moral and mental condition; for reckoning the affliction as equal in extent, *i. e.* the loss of one sense—sight in the one case, and hearing in the other—there is that great difference in its nature. So the deaf and dumb have the advantage over the blind in the use of their physical powers, and the blind have the advantage over the deaf and dumb in their capability of mental development and acquisition of the knowledge of moral principles. This deprivation in the case of the uneducated deaf-mute produces isolation. Having no means of communication with the outer world, they

must *depend upon the eye* for all the knowledge they
can gain of men and things, and while they remain
uneducated this cannot extend beyond the limits of
their own individual experience, In this state they
are unacquainted with their names, ignorant of their
own immortal nature, of the God who made them, of
the Saviour who redeemed them, and of the various
and wonderful works of man. But the blind, on the
contrary, are open to all these intellectual advantages;
though shut out from the light of day, the light of truth
and knowledge can shine into their hearts and
illuminate their path ; and yet their physical infirmity
being greater than that of the deaf and dumb, calls
loudly for sympathy and relief, by putting into their
hands the means by which they may gain a livelihood,
and also acquire knowledge for themslves; as well as
the greater infirmity of the deaf and dumb, affecting
their moral and intellectual advancement, demands for
its relief a medium of intercourse with mankind, by
which they may gain ideas, and become acquainted
with everything that is necessary for their temporal
and eternal welfare.

Dr. Howe, whose experience lay mainly with the
blind, and whose success in educating Laura Bridgman,
the deaf-mute and blind girl, which gained for him
world-wide renown, gave his views on the subject in
his last annual report, which cannot fail to interest the
public generally, as it throws much light on a subject
so little understood.

" I have reflected," says the learned Doctor, "much
in order to decide whether blindness or deafness
(followed, as it must be, by mutism) interferes, most
with a person's happiness, and I have inferred, from
consideration of the sources of happiness and from
acquaintance with many persons of each class, that
deafness is a more formidable obstacle in the way of
normal development, and does necessarily lessen the
amount of human pleasure and enjoyment more than
blindness ; and that, although sight is preferable for
those who have to pursue manual labor fer their own
support, yet hearing, the mother of speech, is far more
important for the development and improvement of
the intellectual and moral faculties, and for the enjoy-

ment which comes from their exercise, and from the
various relations of love and affection. The senses are
the instrumentalities for human development, and for
all moral and intellectual action and reaction among
men. The eye is the key to sensuous enjoyment, and
to a certain range of knowledge of material things; but
the ear is the real queen among the senses, and she
brings us into those moral and social relations and
affections from the indulgence of which the purest,
highest, and most lasting happiness is derived. This
a priori inference is confirmed by pretty extensive
acquaintance with blind persons and with deaf-mutes.
I have found most of the former not only unrepining,
but cheerful, affectionate, confiding and very social;
while most of the latter seem to be always conscious of
a defect or an infirmity, which acts as a bar to intimate
relations with their fellow-men. Speech, in its widest
and best sense, is to them unattainable; and although
the kind of speech which they learn seems marvellous,
and is to some extent pleasurable, but its imperfection
always keeps them in that sort of isolation from other
men in which imperfect knowledge of our language
keeps the foreigner who sojourns among us. We do
not converse freely. He translates his native language
into ours, and we translate ours into his; and much of
the thought and attention of each is occupied in making
the translation. We do not know a foreign language
as we know our vernacular tongue until our thoughts
clothe themselves spontaneously in it; that is until we
think in it and dream in it.

It is indeed a plain fact, and one well known by
teachers of the two classes, that the blind are cheerful,
hopeful, sociable, and confiding, while the deaf-mutes
are inclined to melancholy, to be uncommunicative,
unsocial, jealous, suspicious, and dissatisfied with their
lot in life. It is, indeed, a terribly hard one out of
which to extract that kind of happiness which is "our
being's end and aim."

Besides, the happiness of most persons is greatly
affected by their conventional standing, that is, by the
kind of regard in which they are held by others; and
the blind as well as the deaf are peculiarly sensitive on
this point. It is, indeed, much a matter of convention-

ality, and it differs in different countries, and changes with time, but always exists. The infirmity of blindness is seen and understood instantly by everybody. All pity a blind man, and are eager to show him sympathy. The natural, indeed the best, way to do this is by speech, for by that you express your sympathy. The blind value this sympathy highly, and are ever ready for conversation, although they wish it to be on a footing of equality, and they especially dislike to be considered as objects of charity.

They chat with you, argue with you, joke with you, and enjoy the spirit and fun of conversation as much as you do. Indeed, the chief source of their pleasure in life is intimate oral communication with other persons, and learning their sentiments by words, or else by listening to reading. It will be perceived that the deaf are, to a great extent, necessarily cut off from all this.

The infirmity of the blind strikes you at first sight, and brings pity to your heart and tears to your eyes. But it requires a long time to be fully aware of the extent of the infirmity of the deaf, and much reflection to understand its deplorable nature and effects.

Hundreds and thousands of blind persons are found who are in intimate relations with seeing people, and some in every age have risen to eminence in music, in letters, in legislation, and politics, while there is hardly one deaf-mute whose name is known in history.

Every consideration, and a multitude of instances, show that the infirmity of the blind is lighter than that of the deaf; but in spite of all these the great majority of people if offered the alternative of blindness or deafness and mutism, would unhesitatingly and eagerly accept the latter.

As regards deaf-mutes being inferior to the blind in intellectual achievement, it must be remembered that the art of teaching the former is barely a century old, and has yet hardly passed out of the experimental stage. In fact an efficient method of reaching and training the reasoning faculties of deaf-mutes is still more or less of a desideratum, although progress is being continually

made in this direction, and the time will no doubt
come when with a perfect system it will be possible
for the deaf-mute to vie with those in full possession of
their senses in the intellectual arena; there are very
few good teachers of deaf-mutes new who are not
striving with might and main to attain that happy end.

CHAPTER X.

**History of the Protestant Institution for Deaf-mutes.
—Its Early Struggle.—The First Public Examina-
tion.—The Census Returns of Deaf-mutes in the
Province of Quebec.—Joseph Mackay and the
New Building.**

WHEN the writer of this sketch * took up his residence
at Montreal in the year 1868, there were four schools in
Canada to meet the educational requirements of some
8,500 deaf-mutes scattered over the Dominion, viz:
The two Roman Catholic institutions at Montreal; the
Nova Scotia Institution at Halifax; the Upper Canada
Institution at Hamilton.   The former were the oldest,
having been founded in the year 1848, under the
patronage of the Roman Catholic Bishop of Montreal
and Seminary of St. Sulpice, (the most powerful and
wealthy Roman Catholic corporation in America.)
One of these Roman Catholic Institutions is for boys,
and the Rev. A. Belanger is the principal.   The other
is for girls, and is conducted by the nuns.   The Institution at Halifax was established in August, 1856, and
was long conducted by Principal Hutton.   The
Institution in Upper Canada was begun at Toronto in
1858 by Mr. J. B. McGann, who may be regarded as
the pioneer of deaf-mute instruction in the western part
of the Dominion.   In 1868, Mr. McGann was struggling
manfully to save his school from hopeless bankruptcy
and ruin.   The education of deaf-mutes was a new
departure to the sturdy pioneers of that period in
Western Canada.   Some there were who admitted the
importance of educating deaf-mutes, but doubted its
possibility; others had no objection to the trial being
made, but protested against being taxed to support

---

*This historical sketch was originally written for the *American Annal*,
and has been revised and enlarged for the present work.

"dummies" while at school. The writer could not help sympathizing with Mr. McGann when he said, " I am obliged to buy my fuel on credit, and keep a pass-book with my grocer and baker. My furniture has been twice distrained ·for rent and taxes." Mr. McGann's spare moments were occupied in diffusing information respecting the deaf and dumb, and in convincing the public that their education was not only possible, but absolutely necessary. This, coupled with many examination tours, had the desired effect. The government of Ontario came to Mr. McGann's assistance, and in 1870 opened the present Institution at Belleville, under the direction of Dr. W. J. Palmer who had to resign in September, 1879, and was succeeded by Supt. Mathison.

It will thus be seen that provision was made for the education of deaf-mutes in the western part of the Dominion, in the Maritime Provinces, and for the *Roman Catholic* deaf-mutes in Lower Canada; but *nothing had been done for deaf-mutes of the English-speaking population, or Protestants, in Lower Canada.* Many of these were the descendants of the early settlers, the United-Empire loyalists. None of their deaf-mutes had received any instruction, except in one or two cases, where the parents possessed sufficient means to send them to Hartford or to England for instruction. The writer had not been long a resident in Canada's commercial capital before the necessity of a school for Protestant deaf-mutes was forcibly brought to his notice by the father of one of them, who appealed with sorrowful heart on behalf of his grown-up deaf-mute son, totally uninstructed. Others were soon discovered, some of school age and some past the prime of manhood and womanhood, with no school in the whole Province where their parents could have them taught according to their own religious belief. The writer saw a new field of labor opened for him. His experience for some years as an assistant under the late Dr. Baker, of the Yorkshire Institution for Deaf-mutes, and as a missionary to adult deaf-mutes in different parts of England, amply fitted him for a career of usefulness although surrounded by very great difficulties. A long correspondence on the subjcet of a school for Protestant deaf-mutes in Lower Canada took place in the Montreal *Daily Witness.* Information respecting the numbers of deaf-mutes in the Province was diligently sought for; influential Protestant gentlemen engaged commenced, science and education were consulted, and their aid asked for and obtained. There were no reliable returns of vital statistics published for the Province, and the public seemed to know no more about deaf-mutes and deaf-mute instruction than they did in Ontario when Mr. McGann began his uphill labors. Many doubted the writer's deaf-dumbness on account of the easy way he handled the English language and his literary productions. But it was at last ascertained, as near as could be. that there were about 3500 deaf-mutes in the Dominion, some 1300 being in Lower Canada; and, judging by the relative proportions of Protestant and Roman Catholic populations in the Province, there were probably 200 Protestant deaf-mutes, and of these about 75 were of school age, viz., between 7 and 25 years. (The census returns of Canada of 1870 give Lower Canada 1669 deaf and dumb.)

The information thus gathered and the knowledge on the subject of deaf-mute education possessed by the writer were published in the *Witness.* More correspondence ensued, and several applicants for education were received by the writer. Further inquiry revealed the fact that the provincial legislature of Lower Canada before confederation had voted $80,000 for purposes of education of deaf-mutes, but this sum has not yet been paid out, and the record will probably be all that will now remain in connection with it.

During this correspondence in the public prints, which lasted more than a year, (1868 to 1869,) many of the benovelent Protestants in the city of Montreal, ever alive to the wants of suffering humanity, were quietly watching the issue, and taking notes of the facts brought to light. A few of the most prominent of them came forward and took up the subject. Mr. McGann, then principal of the Ontario Institution at Hamilton, was invited to Montreal to give an exhibition of the progress of some of his pupils, and an address on the subject of deaf-mute instruction; this took place at the close of 1868.

FREDERICK MACKENZIE,

The Hon. Secretary-Treasurer of the Mackay Institution for Protestant Deaf-
Mutes, and a Staunch Friend of Humanity.

On the 7th of January, 1869, a public meeting of those interested in the good work took place in Montreal, and the following prominent Protestant citizens formed themselves into a society to establish an educational institution for Protestant deaf-mutes in Lower Canada :

Ladies.—Mesdames Andrew Allan, P. Redpath, J. W. Dawson, (McGill University,) Major, Bond, Cramp, Fleet, Moffatt, Brydges, Browne, Workman.

Gentlemen.—Mr. Charles Alexander, (president,) Thomas Cramp, (vice-president,) Fred. Mackenzie, (hon. sec.-treas.,) Thos. Workman, John Dougall, (proprietor of the Montreal *Witness*,) Wm. Lunn, G. Moffatt, J. A. Mathewson, J. H. R. Molson, Hon. J. J. C. Abbott, E. Carter, Q C., P. D. Browne, W. H. Benyon, I. F. Barnard, John Leeming, and S. J. Lyman.

With this influential committee great and rapid progress was made, and next day, January 8, another meeting was held. It was resolved to ask for legislative aid and a charter, and to appeal for public subscriptions. Mr. Mackenzie, the secretary-treasurer, reported that he had made diligent inquiries respecting the probable number of Protestant deaf-mutes in the Province, and believed there were over 200. The committee resolved to rent a suitable house and grounds.

At this juncture, Mr. W. H. Van Vliet, mayor of Lacolle, some 40 miles south of Montreal, made an offer to the committee of their choice of three splendid sites for the proposed Institution. Any of these lots would make a very generous donation to any charitable institution; but the committee thought that to remove the Institution so far away would deprive it of the contributions from the benevolent of Montreal, its main source of support.

On the 19th January, 1869, another meeting was held, at which it was reported that the handsome sum of $5,950 had been subscribed, collected chiefly by Mr. Thomas Cramp, the vice-president; the other members of the committee being otherwise engaged, could not then assist in collecting, or the amount would doubtless have been much larger.

G

The work of the hon. secretary-treasurer was no sinecure. He sent out hundreds of circulars to ministers in all parts of the Province to obtain the names, age, sex, circumstances, etc., of all Protestant deaf-mutes in the Province. It may be of interest to the profession to learn how far the circulars succeeded in this mixed community, where the Protestants form only a small minority of the population (about 300,000).

On the 26th January, 250 circulars to Protestant ministers had brought 23 replies, reporting only 5 deaf-mute and 5 blind Protestants.

On the 10th March it was stated that 112 replies to circulars had been received, reporting 38 deaf-mutes, 8 of school age; of 34 blind returned only 5 were of school age. More circulars were sent out.

On April 30th, 210 replies were received, reporting 57 deaf-mutes, 35 males and 22 females. Their ages were: Between 16 and 21 years, 8 males and 5 females, in all 13; between 21 and 30 years, 8, being 4 of each sex.

The committee now wished to know—

1. Between what ages can deaf-mutes receive instruction ?

2. Whether both sexes should be educated together ?

3. Whether the blind and deaf-mutes should be educated together ?

These questions were submitted to several experts, including the writer. All recommended the education of the sexes together, but advised a separate school for the blind, and named the ages at which deaf-mutes could be educated as from 7 to 25 years.

On the 15th December, 1869, another meeting of the committee was held, which the late Rev. Collins Stone of Hartford attended by invitation. He expressed pleasure and satisfaction with his interview with the writer and his testimonials, and recommended them to make a trial with a small school under the management of the writer, with his wife as matron. He kindly offered to allow the writer, and his wife to spend a few months in the Hartford Institution to acquire a knowledge of the system of instruction, if necessary.

He continued to be a warm friend of the Institution up to the time of his lamented death, which took place a few months after his visit to Montreal.

On the 4th May, 1870, another meeting of the committee was held at which there were present Chas. Alexander, the president, John Dougall, Proprietor of the *Daily Witness*, F. Mackenzie, the hon. sec.-treasurer, Dr. Scott, and the writer, and it was unanimously resolved that the writer should at once look for a suitable house and grounds, and open school in September.

THE FIRST PROTESTANT DEAF-MUTE SCHOOL BUILDING.

A house with ample grounds, in a very healthy locality, just outside of the city limits, (Cote St. Antoine,) was obtained in July, at an annual rental of $400, with option of purchase within five years for $8,000, the extent of ground being 58,080 square feet. The house contained accommodation for about 20 pupils, but very scant provision for teachers. The double doors of the parlor were removed, and the room was used as school-room, chapel and sitting-room for the pupils. Baths were put in and a few alterations made, in order that we might make the best of the small accommodation the house afforded.

. At this meeting the committee learned that their
attempt to obtain legislative aid for the school had
failed, but they were not discouraged, and made
another application for a grant, feeling they had the
same right to aid from the State as their Roman
Catholic fellow-citizens had for their Institution. The
government at last made the Institution a grant of
$1,000, which has since been increased to $1,729.

On the 15th September, 1870, the Protestant Institution for Deaf-Mutes opened its doors, for the first
time, for the reception of pupils. During that month
and the following October, 11 pupils, 9 boys and 2 girls,
were admitted. Of these six paid full fees, ($90,) and
five were free.

On the 1st November, 1870, the Institution was
formally opened to the public by the Protestant Bishop
of Montreal and Metropolitan of Canada, in the presence
of an assemblage of prominent ladies and gentlemen, and
another charitable institution was added to the long list
for which Montreal is famous.

During the first session of the new school sixteen
pupils were admitted, thirteen boys and three girls, one
of the latter being a young woman deaf, dumb, and
blind. She was in a most deplorable state. Her
constitution was enfeebled by long confinement and
neglect, and at times she was subject to fits of un-
governable temper; at other times she showed signs
of great intelligence, and some progress was made in
learning the manual alphabet, with the aid of raised
letters, which were procured for her benefit. After
being a few weeks in the Institution she was able to
communicate her wants in signs, and could go about
the house unaided. Her health, however, began to fail,
and her parents contemplating a removal to the West,
and it being found that the Institution in its early
infancy had not the necessary accommodation and staff
of teachers which her case required, her parents were
desired to remove her.

The numerous duties which devolved upon the
principal and matron were such as to require all their
time and constant care from early morning till late at
night. Eight hours a day for six days a week were

spent in the school-room; three hours a day were devoted to teaching different kinds of work about the place, and to training the pupils in habits of industry. Many a night the principal had to sit at the desk attending to correspondence, and the monthly accounts and reports for the meeting of the board of directors. It was, indeed, a year of real hard work, care, and anxiety. The matron, with the aid of a single female cook and the two girls, did all the domestic work of the Institution, and took upon herself the instruction of a class of pupils of a low grade of intellect. The Principal taught two classes and the drawing-class after school-hours, besides acting as teacher of trades, steward, and supervisor. On Sundays a sabbath-school was held, and three hours were devoted to religious instruction by means of the sign-language.

The system of instruction in this Institution is the combined method. Natural signs, writing and the manual alphabet (both single and double-handed) are the chief instruments depended on for teaching. In so small a school great diversity of intellect prevailed, which rendered it necessary to divide the pupils into several classes, and the ingenuity of the teacher was taxed to the utmost to devise methods of reaching the dormant minds of the pupils. Some of its friends suggested that the articulation method as carried on in the excellent school at Northampton, Massachusetts, should be adopted in this Institution, but they soon saw that with such pupils it was an impossibility. The object persistently kept prominently in view during the whole session of the first year, and ever afterwards, has been to give deaf-mutes a knowledge of language (written or otherwise) by whatever methods long experience has suggested as the best and most certain, and to inculcate habits of industry, with moral and religious training.

The public interest in the success of the Institution during the first year was very great, especially towards the close of the session; visitors were numerous, almost daily, which obliged the Principal to leave his classes to show them about the place and answer their questions by the slow process of writing; but the good work was perseveringly continued until the day arrived for the first public examination of the pupils, which was held in the Mechanics' Hall in Montreal on the 13th June, 1871, and was presided over by J. W. Dawson, LL.D., F. R. S., principal of the McGill University. There was a very large audience present, including many of the most prominent men of the city. As this was our first appearance before the public, and many drawbacks had attended the session just then closed, the teachers and pupils felt no small distrust as to the results of their labors. They were, however, so kindly received and assisted by the president of the Institution, (Chas. Alexander,) and the secretary-treasurer, (F. Mackenzie,) that they were encouraged to do their best on the occasion, which was attended with much success. At the close of the exhibition, Dr. Dawson asked the audience to adopt a written recognition of the services rendered by the teachers, and their thorough approval of the system of instruction adopted by the Institution. This proposal was heartily approved by the audience, and the chairman drew up the following words, read them to the audience, and presented them to the writer :

" MR. WIDD :

" The audience desire me to say that they are very much gratified with what they have seen, and desire to encourage you in your good work, and to express their approval of the pupils.

PRINCIPAL DAWSON."

An examination tour through the Province was now resolved on. The secretary-treasurer, F. Mackenzie, Esq., accompanied by the Principal and two of the advanced pupils, visited the largest Protestant towns in the Province, and held public meetings and examinations of the pupils at each place. At all of these places the greatest interest in the work was shown by the public. Collections to defray expenses were taken up at the close of each examination. A very enthusiastic reception was given us at Quebec city, where three of the pupils resided and took part in the examinations. A subscription was immediately taken up to provide the Institution with a printing-press and founts of tpye by a few friends in Quebec and the handsome sum of $267.53 was handed to the secretary-treasurer.

During the following session a lady was engaged as
an assistant teacher, and to instruct semi-mutes in
articulation, which relieved Mrs. Widd, the matron, of
her duties in the school-room, and enabled her to devote
all her time to her own family and the domestic cares
of the Institution. A carpenter was engaged to instruct
the boys in the use of carpentry tools, and the teaching
of printing was undertaken by the Principal. The
reports of the Institution and other matter were
executed by the boys after school hours.

The first session of eight hours daily in the school-
room having proved too exhaustive for the teachers
and too wearisome to the pupils, the time in school
was reduced to *five* hours for five days a week,. and
an hour a day was given to articulation with three or
four promising pupils, and an hour twice a week was
devoted to drawing. This change speedily showed
beneficial results. The health of the pupils and teachers
improved, and their intellectual progress continued to
be quite as satisfactory as previously.

On the 20th January, 1873, the Governor-General of
Canada, Lord Dufferin, and Lady Dufferin visited the
Institution, and conversed with the pupils in the
double-handed alphabet, much to their delight and
surprise.

The board of managers felt the urgent need of larger
and better premises for the Institution, as every year
since the first public examination the number of pupils
admitted into the small house used by the Institution
exceeded 20, and on one occasion there were no less
than 27, besides the principal, matron, assistant teacher,
and two domestic servants, crowded together in the
building, which could only comfortably accommodate
15 at most! Many applications for admission were
refused or postponed. The difficulties of the board
of managers in raising funds to meet current expenses
were very great, the Institution having to depend for
support on public subscriptions, the fees of paying
pupils, and the $1,000 grant made by the provincial
legislature, which all together were never sufficient to
keep the Institution from debt by current expenses.
The salaries of the teachers (principal and matron
included) did not exceed $600 a year, and the utmost

Interior View of the Deaf-mute School-room (old building)—Mr. Widd Teaching the Significance of Words.

CHARLES ALEXANDER,

The First President of the Mackay Institution for Protestant Deaf-Mutes, and the
Steadfast Friend of the Poor and Unfortunate.

economy and frugality were practised in all expenditures. Still, the finances of the Institution continued in rather an unsatisfactory state. The managers tried from time to time to raise funds for enlarging the building, or to buy more land and build elsewhere. One lady manager, Mrs. C. J. Brydges, whose active benevolence is well known in Canada, managed with no small trouble to collect $2,061 towards a building fund; another, Mrs. P. Holland, collected $500 for the same object, and others of the board of managers exerted themselves in the same direction; but not much success attended their efforts on account of great financial depression which prevailed at the time.

The census returns of Lower Canada were published in 1873-'4, and showed a total of 1669 deaf-mutes—883 males and 786 females; but every attempt to find the number of those who were of Protestant parentage failed, and these returns proved of comparatively little value to the Institution. New cases of Protestant deaf-mutes continued to be reported to the principal and president of the Institution, but nothing particular was done to induce them to enter the Institution on account of its financial condition and the want of proper accommodation.

Matters became worse in 1876, when failures in trade and financial depression were universal. The Institution was without funds and much in debt. The prospects of a larger building and better times were to all appearance as far off as ever. The managers felt much discouraged, and to keep the Institution going the secretary-treasurer and the president advanced money from their private funds. As the dark cloud gathered over the prospects of the future of the Institution, and " while we were trying," as the worthy president of the Institution stated at the last annual meeting, " to make both ends meet, in the time of our anxiety God raised up a friend to help us in the very way we wished—that is, to extend our efforts by means of a larger building—and put it into the heart of an old and respected fellow-citizen, Joseph Mackay, Esq., to give us a splendid piece of land, and to erect thereon at his own expense a stone building capable of accommodating 80 pupils and their teachers."

H

THE MACKAY INSTITUTION FOR PROTESTANT DEAF-MUTES, MONTREAL.

The corner-stone of this magnificent gift was laid on the 6th June, 1877, in the presence of a large number of ladies and gentlemen, on which occasion this kind and Christian friend of the deaf and dumb—who will ever keep his name in grateful remembrance—addressed the assembly as follows:

" Mr. Chairman, Ladies and Gentlemen : The Institution for which this building is being erected has had as yet a brief career of usefulness. Among its founders and friends may be numbered leading citizens of Montreal, besides ladies and gentlemen, and I think special mention should be made in this connection of our worthy chairman, Mr. Charles Alexander, our secretary-treasurer, Mr. F. Mackenzie ; Mr. Thomas Cramp, Mr. Andrew Allen, Mr. Dougall, senior, who is always doing good wherever he goes, Mr. Widd, the principal of the school, as well as the governors and managers, who have done good work. The work of the school was commenced in 1870, with sixteen pupils ; the largest number yet in attendance was twenty-five, during the session of 1874 and 1875. The total number connected with the school from its formation is forty-one ; some of these have continued through several sessions, and others have remained for only a few months. Of the twenty-two in attendance last session, seven have paid full fees, five partial fees, ten were free pupils. Of the education given, it may be sufficient for me to say that it is under the able and judicious direction of the principal and his assistant, and embraces intellectual and spiritual culture, as well as instruction in several of the useful arts of life. The pupils are prepared, when they remain a sufficient time in the Institution, to make their way in this world, and have their minds and hearts turned to the higher realities of the world to come. What a blessing to the afflicted ! And thus the founders and supporters are made a blessing, as stewards of God's bounty. The government of our Province has given a small annual grant in aid of the Institution, but its support has been chiefly drawn from private benevolence. Feeling deeply the importance and value of the work done, and wishing to promote its success and extension. I resolved some time ago, as announced in a letter

addressed to you, Mr. Chairman, on the 24th of November last, to erect this building, and to place it and
the ground attached to it in the hands of trustees, to
be used by them and their successors for the education
of the Protestant deaf and dumb of this Province.
Several conversations with Mr. Widd, who spoke of
the immediate necessity of larger buildings, and the
difficulties in obtaining funds, led to this decision,
especially when on mentioning it to a relative, the reply
was ' Why not do it yourself?'   I only add, that I trust
and pray this building may be completed without any
accident or untoward incident, and be carried to a
speedy and successful completion; and for years and
generations to come the Institution may, through the
Divine favor, prove a source of manifold blessing to the
afflicted class whose good it seeks, and may never lack
generous, warm-hearted friends, and wise and godly
instructors to carry on the work."

The board of managers resolved, as a token of their
gratitude to Mr. Mackay for his noble gift, to change
the name of the Institution to " The Mackay Institution
for Protestant Deaf-Mutes."   It is erected on one of the
most picturesque sites on the Island of Montreal com-
manding a view of the St. Lawrence, the Mountain,
being visible from so many points, being situated on
Cote St. Luc road.   It was originally intended to erect
a building to accommodate about 50 pupils, but after
much careful thought and study, Mr. Mackay decided
to construct a much large building, to accommodate
from 80 to 100.   The style of the building is Gothic,
having four facades rock-faced courses, with trimmings
and openings, water-table belts, courses, and bands of
cut stone.   The building is 95 by 50, and three
stories in height, having a well elevated basement and
mansard roof, ornamented.   There are two towers,
one at each end, and the main entrance is in the
centre, with a handsome flight of stone steps, portico,
etc.   The basement is 10 feet high; the floor being
level with the ground, will afford abundance of light
and air.   There are three entrances; one on the north
side for baker, butcher, etc.; and one for girls and one
for boys to the play-ground, with doors opening into
the hall and wide corridor, and refectory 43 by 20,

with openings on three sides, with serving-room,
teachers' dining-room, kitchen, scullery, laundry,
larder, cook's pantry, store-room, lavatories, fuel cellar,
and two boilers for heating the building with hot
water. The ground floor is 15 feet high, and
contains an octagonal vestibule 12 feet in diameter,
opening to a hall 20 by 14, having a handsome staircase six feet in width in the centre, and two returns of
four feet. On the left are two rooms, a class-room
87.7 by 25, and the boys' recreation-room 37-6 by 16.
Both these rooms can be made one for meetings, etc.,
by sliding the doors out of the way which divide them.
On the right is the office and board-room, with safe,
16.6 by 16, and teacher's room, 28 by 26, and corridor
between them, with staircase and private entrance
leading into the girls' recreation-room in front, 20 by
16, and in rear a class room 19 by 16. The
second story is 12 ft. 6 in. high, and contains a
library 18 by 12, two bedrooms, or dormitories, each
16 by 16, and ten bedrooms, each 11 by 16, girls, and
boys' lavatories, hall in the centre, with corridor 8 ft.
in width, and staircase at each end. The third
story is 12 ft. 6 in. high, and contains dormitories,
hospitals, and lavatories, nurse's rooms galleries, etc.
To secure thorough ventilation and warming, the
ventilating and smoke flues, each 3 by 2 ft., are
carried up through the centre of the building, with
register at the floor and ceiling on each story. The
heating apparatus consists of two of Spence's hot
water boilers, connected so that they can be worked
separate or together, with coils in all the rooms,
halls, corridors, dormitories, etc. The work, which
is of the most substantial character, was designed and
carried out under the superintendence of John James
Browne, a Montreal architect.

CHAPTER XI.

Opening of the Mackay Institution by Lord and Lady
Dufferin.—The Ninth Annual General Meeting.—
Congratulatory Address.—Deaf-mutes at Divine
Service.—Press Notices.—To Parents of Deaf-
mutes.—The Audiphone, &c.—An Appeal for the
Deaf-mute.

THE new Institution building was formally opened on
the 12th February, 1878, by Lord Dufferin, the late
Governor-General of Canada, in the presence of a
brilliant assembly. Among whom were the Hon. Mr.
Letellier, the late Lieutenant-Governor of Quebec, His
Lordship the Metropolitan of Canada, Bishop Oxenden,
Dr. Dawson, Principal of McGill University, Lieut.-
General Smyth, U. S. Consul-General Dart, C. J.
Brydges, Chas. Alexander, Alderman Clendinneng,
Capt. Smyth, Joseph Mackay, Edward Mackay, Rev.
Dr. De Sola, Col. Dyde, and about 400 others. The
Institution was very tastefully and elaborately decorated
for the occasion. Mr. Joseph Mackay made the deed
of donation with a few appropriate remarks.

An address was read to Lord Dufferin by Mr. Charles
Alexander, the president, welcoming him as the patron
of the Institution. An address of welcome from the
pupils was also read, and one of the pupils, Miss Jessie
Macfarlane, presented a bouquet of beautiful flowers
to Lady Dufferin, who smiled pleasantly, stooping
down to receive it.

Lord Dufferin, the patron, made a very appropriate
reply to the addresses, praising Mr. Mackay's liberality,
and contrasting the former establishment which he
had visited some years before, with the present fine
building. He then declared the Institution opened for
the purposes for which it was erected, and the visitors
took their departure after inspecting the building.

The ninth annual general meeting of the Institution
was held on the 23rd October, 1879, Mr. Joseph

Mackay, the president and founder, after whom the Institute is named, occupied the chair. Amongst other friends of the Institute present were His Lordship the Bishop of Montreal, Messrs. C. J. Brydges, Fred. Mackenzie, Honorary Secretary, Charles Alexander, A. W. Ogilvie, John Sterling, F. W. Thomas, Revs. Messrs. Johnson, Stevenson, Canon Norman, Lindsay, Principal MacVicar, and Principal Dawson, of McGill College, and Dr. Scott.

The proceedings were opened with prayer, after which the President, in opening the meeting, said:

Ladies and Gentlemen :—The Managers of this Institution have much pleasure in meeting the friends of the deaf and dumb, on this the ninth anniversary, to hear the report of the past year and to make resolves for the future. Since we last met here education has been going on steadily under Mr. Widd's able management. Indeed, to my knowledge, this is the only Institution where a deaf-mute occupies the position of Principal, filling the office with satisfaction to the Board. We have at length been able to secure the services of a lady teacher of articulation, Miss Littlefield, of Boston, who, we are assured, will be a valuable addition to the staff. We have much reason for thankfulness for the measure of support this Institution receives and the interest evinced in its success, yet a large increase is necessary if we would continue this valuable work, remembering we have no endowment fund and only a small Government grant, together with some pupils' fees, to meet our increasing expenditure, and whilst giving your means let me urge you to visit the Institution to see for yourselves the progress made, and to give encouragement to the teachers. We have here three children from one family and a fourth to come. What sacrifice would not any of you make to restore speech and hearing to an afflicted child of your own? Then, as a thank-offering for these gifts Providence has bestowed on you, increase your liberality. We had hoped to have been able to put up workshops much required, indeed had plans ready and tenders received, but had to abandon them, and instead ended our financial year, unfortunately, with a deficit. In view of this, our Managers resolved that our Principal should visit the Townships and personally solicit subscriptions. His success was gratifying, considering the universal depression, and we believe he has created an interest which will be permanent. We have to thank our friends in Quebec, as well as in the Eastern Townships, for their valuable contributions. I will now call on our Honorary Secretary to read the reports.

The Secretary-Treasurer, F. MACKENZIE, then read the Financial Statement, the Annual Reports of the Board of Managers, of the Principal, and that of the Examiner of the School, the Rev. Canon Norman, M.A., D.C.L., all of which will be found in the Report of the Institution.

The Teacher of Articulation, Miss Littlefield, of Boston, Mass., gave an exhibition of the results of six weeks, instruction in articulation by Bell's Visible Speech, which was highly gratifying, being in every instance very creditable. It was intended also to have an examination of the pupils generally, but as the time was so limited and there was a large amount of business before the meeting it was dispensed with.

The usual resolutions on such occasions were put and passed, and eloquent speeches were delivered by Rev. Hugh Johnstone, Principal Dawson, Rev. Mr. Stevenson, Rev. Canon Norman, A. W. Ogilvie, Esq., and others. The pupils then gave "God Save the Queen," in the sign-language, and the benediction closed the proceedings. The visitors then inspected the work of the pupils and the building generally, and expressed themselves thoroughly satisfied with everything.

The following address from the pupils to Mr. Widd was read to the audience by the Secretary-Treasurer, while Mr. John Macnaughton read it on his fingers to Mr. Widd. It was then handed to him by the President, Mr. Mackay. Mr. Widd made a very suitable and feeling reply in the sign-language. The address was beautifully got up in colors and penmanship by Mr. Macnaughton, the border being made up of the prettiest autumnal maple leaves, painted in all their gorgeous colors, and was very much admired, both as a work of art and for the sentiments it expressed :—

THOMAS WIDD,

The Principal of the Mackay Institution for Protestant Deaf-Mutes.

Mr. Widd became totally deaf. and consequently dumb, between the ages of three and four years by scarlet fever. He was edicated in the Yerkshire Institution for the Deaf and Dumb at Doncaster, under Dr. Baker. where he also received his valuable training as a teacher. He was for some years employed as a missionary to the deaf and dumb in various parts of England, and founded associations for the moral and religious instruction of the adult deaf and dumb in Sheffield and other English towns. In 1867 he came to Canada to ameliorate the condition of his afflicted brethren in that country. The results of his efforts are to be seen in the substantial building erected by Mr. Joseph Mackay for the instruction of Protestant deaf-mutes in Lower Canada.

" *TO MR. THOMAS WIDD:*

" *Dear Teacher and Guide,—Permit us, your affectionate*
" *and grateful pupils, to congratulate you on your entrance*
" *upon your tenth year of principalship of the Institution*
" *for the instruction of Protestant Deaf-mutes of the*
" *Province of Quebec, and pray God to bless you with*
" *health and strength to continue your noble and self-denying*
" *labors for many years to come. You have dispelled the*
" *gloom of intellectual night in which we long lay groping,*
" *and brought us into the broad sunlight of knowledge.*
" *How well you have performed your work of educating us*
" *let our progress and proficiency attest. With kind and*
" *loving hand you have led us step by step on our path to*
" *knowledge, with patience borne with our waywardness,*
" *and firmly, yet gently, you have corrected our errors and*
" *shortcomings. We gratefully acknowledge all the good*
" *you have done us, and pray God to reward you, for we*
" *cannot. Our limited knowledge of language fails to*
" *adequately describe the extent of our respect and affection*
" *toward you, our dear and honored teacher. Therefore we*
" *beg you to accept our hearty congratulations.*

" *JOHN MACNAUGHTON,*

" *In the name of my fellow pupils.*"

"*Mackay Institution for Protestant Deaf-Mutes,*
"*Montreal,* 23rd October, 1879."

The following is an address from Mr. J. Outterson, a former pupil of the Institution, who happened to be in Montreal on a visit, and wished to say a few words expressing his gratitude for benefits received in the Institution:

"*Mr. Chairman, Ladies and Gentlemen.*

" As an old pupil of this Institution, allow me to make a few remarks upon the benefits I have derived from the admirable system of education pursued in it. When I compare my former state and condition before I became a pupil with my present, I am filled with amazement and wonder, and consider myself a new

I

man lifted into a new world. I can now take my place in society and hold converse without difficulty with any one. I can now read my Bible with an intelligent and thankful appreciation of its blessed truths.

" I and all Protestant deaf-mutes of the Province of Quebec have great reason to bless and thank Him, ' who hath formed both tongue and ear,' for bringing Mr. Widd across the Atlantic from England to found this admirable Institution (my *alma mater*, I am proud to say), and putting it into the hearts of you, Mr. Chairman, Ladies and Gentlemen of the Board of Managers, to stand by him, and cheer him on by your counsels and pecuniary assistance and support.

" Having myself been benefited so much, I feel very anxious that all my fellow Protestant mutes of this Province should also share in its benefits. I would suggest that a more energetic effort be made to raise funds throughout the Province, so as to admit more pupils by bringing its claims more and more before the benevolent and charitable public. I shall always be happy to do all in my power to aid the school."

The following account of Divine Service in the Mackay Institution is from the *Argenteuil Advertiser* (Lachute), of Dec. 17th, 1879, and will give some idea how the Sabbath is spent by Protestant deaf-mutes at that school:

" On Sunday, the 14th of December, we had the pleasure of being present at and witnessing divine service amongst the pupils of the Mackay Institute for deaf-mutes, Cote St. Luc Road, Montreal. Our readers are aware that through the munificent liberality of Joseph Mackay, Esq., a palatial building has been erected for the education and training of the Protestant deaf and dumb of the Province of Quebec, where some thirty or forty children are acquiring an education which will fit them to become useful members of society. Not only is the secular education of the pupils attained in this institution, but their moral and religious training is also carefully attended to. Every

Sabbath afternoon divine worship, in the sign language, is held in the school-room, conducted by Mr. Principal Widd. The service is open to adult deaf-mutes, as well as to the pupils of the Mackay Institute, on the occasion above referred to, the mute congregation assembled in the school-room. The order of service was written on the black-board, and a Bible lay on the desks before each pupil. It was plain to see from the expression which pervaded each countenance that all were fully conscious of the solemnity of the occasion. At three o'clock Principal Widd took his stand, and the congregation rising, he spelled on his fingers, verse by verse, the lxvii. Psalm, (*Deus Misereatur*) explaining also by pantomime, or signs, the meaning of each verse as he proceeded, so that the youngest pupil could not fail to understand; then was given by minister and congregation, the Lord's Prayer, in sign language, and so graphic were the gestures that one totally unacquainted with this style of language, could not fail to understand the meaning of the signs made. This was followed by the spelling (reading, shall we say) of the lxxxii. Psalm, as lesson, also translated into pantomime. Then followed the Second and Third Collects of the Evening Service. After this a short sermon was preached, of which we give a condensed report. Principal Widd took for his text " How excellent is thy loving-kindness, O God," (Ps. xxxvi., 7) and then in graphic pantomime, said :

" God's greatest and most excellent attribute is love. It is made manifest to us in all His works—in the light which surrounds us, in the air we breathe, in the food which He causes the earth to bring forth abundantly for our sustenance. Like as a loving earthly father cares for and provides for his children, so does our Heavenly Father care for us. His watchful care preserves us also from all dangers, both seen and unseen. His greatest love, however, is made manifest in the gift of His Son Jesus Christ, who was offered up a sacrifice in our stead,—who died for our sins, and who is now our Intercessor before the Throne of God. We ought all to love God, because he has manifested His love for us in so gracious and effectual a manner; and if we do love Him we shall exemplify it in our

daily lives, by our praises to Him and obedience to
His word and His laws; we shall hate sin, and love
the good; we shall study His holy word, the Scriptures,
daily, and shape our lives in accordance with their
holy lessons. But if we say we love God and do not
obey His laws, then He will regard us as hypocrites,
and will most surely punish us. His mercy is everlast-
ing, His power infinite, and He will ever listen to our
prayer for help. Let us, therefore, to-day raise our
thoughts in love to God, the Father in that He gave
His Son Jesus Christ to be an offering in our behalf,
and let us pray the Holy Ghost to shed upon us His
benign influence, which alone can make our lives
worthy the name of Christians. Above all, let us ever
remember with devout gratitude, the grand old truth
contained in our text, which ascribes the perfection of
excellence to the loving-kindness of God."

"It was touching to witness the play of expression
which flitted over the faces of his congregation, as the
preacher proceeded with his discourse. There was
absolute silence, not a word spoken or a sound uttered;
yet the audience (if we may use the word) received
advice, warning, encouragement. It was a scene of
great interest, and one of which but few hearing and
speaking persons can imagine the importance. The
service was concluded with the benediction, having
lasted about one hour."

———

The Montreal *Witness*; of Dec. 12th, 1879, contains
the following article regarding the intellectual and
industrial training of youth :

" The educators of deaf-mutes have discovered, earlier than those who
have the training of youth who have all their powers, that the best results
are attained by the training of the constructive along with the intellectual
faculties. It is only by degrees that most educationists are learning that
man's work upon the face of the world is done with his hands and that his
happiness and usefulness are both very much curtailed by the suppression
of the faculties which prompt to manual work. Drawing is perhaps the
best, although by no means the only form in which the use of the hands
can be introduced into schools, and this is happily now a part of the course
in the schools of Montreal. We hope to see the day when Kindergarten
exercises will form a part of all early school training, to be followed in
later years by some form of constructive labor which shall occupy a good

part of the time. We know some who send their boys to practise a trade if only for an hour or so daily. This course is to be much commended. It is quite usual in Germany, where even Royal and Imperial princes learn trades. Mr. Widd, Principal of the Mackay Institute, makes an earnest appeal for workshops in which to educate his pupils to trades. The printers' trade is the only one which is at present taught there. He points out that it is very hard to get situations for deaf-mute boys who have no trade. Employers shrink from the work of teaching them, but like to get them as journeymen after they have learned. Another consideration, and this one applies also to those who have all their faculties, is that the period of a mental education has to terminate early for those who have still to learn their trade, and might last much longer if the trade was being acquired at the same time, or at least the faculties required in mechanical operations being trained. We hope the necessary funds for establishing these workshops will not be lacking."

In noticing the historical sketch of the Mackay Institution in the *American Annals of the Deaf and Dumb*, October, 1877, the Editor of the *Deaf-mute Journal* of New York says :—

"One cannot pick up the October *Annals*, look at the fine building in the frontispiece, and then read the accompanying account of the Mackay Institution for Protestant Deaf-mutes without the conviction that now and then a deaf-mute does not live in vain. Mr. Thomas Widd, the Principal of the Institution, is a deaf-mute, and the only deaf-mute principal of an institution of that kind in America. There are two or three principals of day schools, but only one of an institution.

"Going to Canada late in the sixties, Thomas Widd toiled a couple of years in that deserted field before he could arouse enough enthusiasm to make a beginning. And when he did, and managed to live from year to year, slowly increasing his little flock the while, well-nigh his only resource was individual charity. Our annals hardly present a parallel of such work, the present enlightement and the numerous flourishing examples all considered. In his brief history of the institution, he tells us that he worked eight hours a day in the school-room, he taught two classes out of school hours, he was principal, steward, supervisor, and teacher of trades, and the hours of night were diligently utilized to complete such duties as the day required. He had to house, in a building comfortably accommodating but fifteen, besides himself, one teacher and two domestics, twenty, and at one time twenty-seven pupils. And as to finances and salaried rewards, the matron, teachers and himself between them, got the immense aggregate of $600 a year! But Thomas Widd is a deaf-mute, and is working for the good of other deaf-mutes. Incidentally, he tells us that circumstances at first compelled him to use the eight-hour system, but as soon as he could, with commendably alacrity, he discarded it and sub-

stituted five hours, which change speedily showed beneficial results in the
health and improvement of the pupils, and the physique of the teachers
improved also.

"In the fall of 1876, a citizen of Montreal, Joseph Mackay, Esq., who
had long been watching the course of the institution and the labors of Mr.
Widd, came forward and said he would erect a building of stone on a fine
plot of ground, capable of accommodating 80 pupils, with the necessary
officers. This has been done, and the structure is now ready for occupation.

"We fail to recall a parellel case in deaf-mute institutions anywhere.
The fine Clark Institution, tn Northampton, Mass, owes its prosperity to
the munificence of a gentleman whose name it bears; but the money came
as a legacy, bestowed when the owner had no further use for it. Besides,
it was given to promote the interests of a peculiar system—that of
articulation. Mr. Mackay is alive and can daily see the fruits of his good
deed. His benevolence is not marred by any hobby, but is a generous,
whole-souled help, and, if length of days is a boon to be coveted, may he
live a number of years equal to the dollars he has given

"The facts as they are, are very suggestive. Mr. Widd is the only deaf-
mute principal of an institution, as far as we know, and that institution, of
all others, has been favored in an unparalleled way, in a country, too, where
such things are rarely looked for. The instance stands out brightly in a
back-ground that increases its proportions—it adds one more triumph to
the few vouchsafed to deaf-mutes."

To Parents of Deaf-mutes.—When parents
discover that their child does not seem to hear
or to try to talk like ordinary children, they begin
to suspect that it is deaf and dumb, and search
for the best remedy they can find for such afflictions.
Deafness is one of the most difficult to cure of human
ailments, and there is probably not a single genuine
cure of total deafness on record. Unprincipled
professional men and quack doctors have paid special
attention to cases of deafness and reaped an abundant
harvest. They have made the partially deaf totally
deaf, and those in whose cases existed no hope whatever
have been made to undergo untold suffering and great
pecuniary loss.

In nearly every case of the pupils in the Mackay
Institution (including all those admitted since 1870),
quack and other remedies have been resorted to for
the recovery of hearing, but without the slightest
benefit. In the case of total deafness from protracted

illness or accident, it is always found that the auditory nerve is either paralysed or destroyed, and nothing short of a miracle can effect a cure. The wisest and only safe course to pursue in all cases of deafness in children or adults is to consult a reliable and respectable physician and follow his advice.

The veteran teacher of deaf-mutes and founder of the Ontario Institution, Mr. J. B. McGann, gives his testimony on this subject (which coincides with that of every other person of experience with deaf-mutes), as follows:

" In my travels in Ontario, I found that in nine cases out of ten quack remedies have been applied to effect the restoration of hearing and of speech. Some of these remedies proved to have been of a very painful nature in their operation—others harmless and absurd, and all without any beneficial results. I have yet to learn, notwithstanding the rigorous process of scientific investigation which marks the 19th century, that there is a cureable property for the congenitally deaf. Dr. Wilde, the distinguished Aurist, Dublin, writes in his treatise on the ear, thus: ' *Except by miraculous interference*, I do not believe that the true congenital mute was ever made to hear, and those who lose their hearing so early in life as never to have acquired speech, come into the same category.' Dr. Stand, the eminent Physician of the Royal Institution for the Deaf and Dumb, Paris, who made more *post mortem* examinations to ascertain the cause of deafness than any other man, says, 'That in most cases of profound deafness the cause was paralysis of the auditory nerve—the nerve of hearing was *dead, and medical means have no effect on the dead.*' "

Early in 1879 an instrument called the AUDIPHONE was invented in Chicago to enable the deaf to hear and the dumb to speak. It made a few persons, who were only *slightly deaf*, hear better, and straightway the news flew to every quarter of the world that the deaf would be no longer deaf and the dumb no longer dumb, and that schools for deaf-mutes were things of the past. The inventor of this creation of science no doubt reaped a large harvest by its sale. Many purchased it only to be sadly disappointed and

to mourn the loss of their money; others felt slight
vibrations of sound by the help of the instrument and
imagined they could hear; but as far as can be learned,
the number of those who have found the audiphone of
any use are very few and far between, and those are
persons who have but very slight deafness. Those
inventions profess to make the totally deaf hear, which
is as absurd a statement as to say that spectacles can
make the blind see! The Audiphone had scarcely been
in the market six months before the DENTIPHONE and
the TANGIPHONE appeared, and claimed to be able to
do even greater wonders than their predecessor. The
MAGNIPHONE, by Prof. Hughes, is another wonderful
invention, which, we believe, appeared before the
Audiphone. It claims to enable a person (not deaf, of
course), to hear the foot steps of a fly on a table, or the
touch of a hair when rubbed against a pen. This
instrument is probably the best and most valuable that
has been invented to aid the ear, but the inventor is
more honest and does not profess to be able to aid the
totally deaf by the instrument. Speaking on this
subject, the Editor of the Toronto *Silent World* remarks:

" We fully endorse Mr. Widd's opinion with regard to
the Audiphone. We have little doubt that the so-called
invention is a mere catch-penny device for extracting
money from the pockets of the credulous. A moment's
consideration will show that to hear a sound correctly
is a very different thing from merely hearing a sound
simply because it is loud, and similiarly, to feel a
vibration with the teeth is a very different thing to
distinguishing the nature and quality of such vibration,
which is absolutely necessary to give any value to it
as a conveyance of language. To put a parallel case:
If a mirror is cracked through in every direction, or if
it be rubbed over with whiting, no light will ever
make it take a correct image of any object; it might
catch in the first instance a vague fragmentary reflection, in the other a dull gloom, but for any practical
purpose as a mirror it is absolutely useless. If any
invention were to be of any service at all, it would be
the Magniphone of Professor Hughes, which is said to
enable a person to hear the sound of a fly's foot on a
board, or the crackling of a feather rubbed against a

JOHN DOUGALL, Senr.,

The Proprietor of the Montreal and New York DAILY WITNESS. The earliest and most staunch friend and advocate of Mr. Widd, to whom he is under many great obligations for his wise counsels and kind encouragement in his struggle to start the Institution for Protestant deaf-mutes in the Province of Quebec.

stick. But inasmuch as the deaf-mute has not in himself the right form of apparatus, or there is some part
of it wanting, neither this nor any other form of
magnifying sound or conveying it to the auditory
nerve has ever been devised that will benefit deaf-
mutes, or is likely to be until the resources of science
shall enable physicians to construct by artificial means,
and insert into the cavity of the ear such appliances as
will supply the parts wanting either from congenital
causes or from ravages of disease. A very unlikely
thing in our opinion to happen, but an absolute *sine
qua non* to hearing with the least correctness."

AN APPEAL FOR THE DEAF-MUTE.

[The following beautiful appeal, written for " Diogenes," a comic paper published
in Montreal about twelve years ago, has been the means of obtaining many
kind friends for deaf-mutes and supporters of their schools. The name of the
author is unknown.]

Deaf! Not a murmur or a loving word
Can ever reach his ear. The raging sea,
The pealing thunder, and the cannon's roar
To him are silent—silent as the grave.
Not quite : for, ever, when God takes away
He gives in other shape. The tramp of feet,
The crash of falling things. the waves of sound
Strike on a deaf man's feeling with a force
To us unknown. Vibrations of the air
Play through his frame, on sympathetic nerves
Like fine-strung instruments of varied tone.

Dumb! Not a murmur or a loving word
Can ever pass his lip. The cry of rage,
The voice of friendship, and the vows of love
Freeze on his tongue, so impotent of sound.

But deem not that intelligence is null
In that doomed mortal. Gaze upon his eye—
A speaking eye!—an eye that seems to hear
E'en by observing, and that gathers more
From flickering lights and shadows of a face
Than duller minds can gain from spoken words.
The age of miracles hath past ; but man
Can summon art and science to his aid,
And cause the faculties of sight and touch
To act imperfectly for speech and ear.

J

The deaf-mute seems, by Nature, formed to be
A delicate artificer, and skilled
In subtle operations of the hand.
He can be taught to read, and thus to learn
The story of the Present or the Past,
Or by quick signs to share his inmost thoughts
Chiefly for those for whom he yearneth most,
His fellow suff'rers!   Nay, it sometimes haps
That men, like Kitto,   'reft of senses twain,
Have, by their lore, electrified the world,
And won the crown of literary fame.

Spare not your gifts, ye wealthy of the land,
To these afflicted brethren.   Ye to whom
Heav'n grants that sweetest of all blessings, health,
And the keen joys of each corporeal sense,
Aid those to whom these blessings are denied,
And shed some sunshine o'er their gloomy lives.
Let us all tread, as closely as we can,
In the blest footprints of that Holy One
Who went about, forever doing good,
Making the dumb to speak, the deaf to hear.

CHAPTER XII.

An Easy Method of Teaching Deaf-mutes at Home.

FOR the benefit of those who desire to do all they can
to instruct their own children before sending them to
an Institution, the following description has been
prepared of the method to be pursued.   It is hoped
that all having mute children will spare no pains in
their home instruction, and however little progress
may be secured, it will still be of value to the child.
In some cases, it may be weeks, or months, before the
child is able to write a single word, but if the plan
here explained is perseveringly carried out, success
is certain.

The method here presented is not a new one: it has
been in vogue more than half a century, and is still
used with great success by some of the best instructors
of deaf-mutes.

In addition to writing words and sentences, let the
child also spell them by means of the manual alphabet,
of which engravings are given in this book.

In memorizing the alphabets, the best way is to learn thoroughly each horizontal row of characters before commencing the next one below. If this is done, the alphabet will be perfectly mastered in less than an hour. Use either the one or the two handed alphabets as you like best.

It is also well to use every means to preserve the vocal utterance of the child, for, though hearing cannot be recovered, speech may, in many cases, be retained, if the child is constantly practised in the use of its voice.

The child may be taught as early as the age of three or four to write a few words. From that age, until six or seven, he should be practised by the method here given, and then sent to some institution, where his progress will be very rapid if this preparatory home training has been well performed.

HOW TO BEGIN.—FIRST STEP.

Begin by writing in a plain round hand the name of some common object. Show to the child first the object and then the name, pointing from one to the other until he sees that the name stands for the object. Get him to copy the word, and when he has mastered it, teach him another in the same way. Always write *the* before the names of objects. As above explained teach the following list of words containing all the letters of the alphabet:

the book,	**the cup,**	**the mug,**	**the jar,**
the key,	**the quill,**	**the feather,**	**the box,**
the pen,	**the watch,**	**the glove,**	**the zinc.**

Besides these, the names father, mother, the child's own name, and those of his brothers and sisters, should be taught.

SENTENCES.

As soon as the child can write the names of five or six objects, sentences may be taught. To do this a short direction to do something, as, *Touch the box,* is shown to the pupil. Then the teacher himself touches the box and gets the child to imitate him. After several repetitions the child is made to copy the sentence, *I touched the box,* as the proper way of expressing what he has done. He is then directed in writing to touch some other object of which he knows the name, and, if he does not understand, the teacher again explains as before. This is repeated frequently until the pupil, on being shown a direction to touch a familiar object, will at once go and do so. This process of writing a short direction, showing the child what it means by simply performing the action indicated, and then having him copy the proper form of sentence to express what he has done, is to be always carried out. Proceed in the same manner with many examples like the following:

Touch the key.   Touch the table.
Touch the cup.   Touch the chair.
Touch the mug.   Touch father.
Touch the jar.   Touch mother.
Touch the zinc.   Touch John.
Touch the watch.   Touch Mary.

The teacher must also touch objects himself, and get the child to describe what he has done, by using *you* in place of *I*, thus:

You touched the key.   You touched the fork.
You touched the shovel.   You touched the glove.

A third person should also be asked to do something in the presence of the child, and the latter taught to describe it, as:

Father touched the slate.   John touched the fan.
Mother touched the pail.   Mary touched the jug.
John touched Mary.   Mary touched John.

When the pupil has became expert in these exercises, direct him to touch two or more objects, which must at first be placed together before him. Vary all of the foregoing exercises, as in the examples given below:

I touched the hat and the key.
I touched the chair and the table.
You touched the book and the shovel.
You touched the pencil and the slate.
Father touched the door and the hat.
John touched the knife and the fork.

The same exercises should now be continued, with the following words in place of *touch*. Each word must be used quite often and thoroughly mastered before a new one is given:

bring,	open,	shut.	kick,	strike,	throw,
hit,	push,	pull,	gather,	break,	pare,
tear,	cut,	lift,	bite,	wash,	wipe,
sweep,	eat,	drink,	smell,	taste,	slap,
clean,	whip,	raise,	pat,	rub,	drop,
bind,	shake,	roll,	pinch,	lock,	unlock,
cover,	uncover,	toss,	fill,	empty,	scrape,
feed,	light,	punch,	tickle,	comb,	scratch,

PHRASES.

The following phrases, it will be seen, are as easily explained as any of the single words above given, by merely performing the act indicated. These should be used very often, and with as many objects as are appropriate to them :

> sit on, stand on, lie on, kneel on, write on, play on, run on, jump on, roll on, stand in, stand under, walk to, go into, walk into, run into, go out of, walk out of, run out of, put on, take off, jump over, stand before, stand behind, stand beside, stand near, walk around, walk across, stand between, point to, bow to, shake hands.

The following examples will show how the above phrases are to be used :

I sat on the chair.	I stood in the tub.
I stood on the box.	I blew out the match.
I went to the table.	I walked to the gate.
You ran on the grass.	You went into the house.
You turned off the gas.	You jumped over the stool.
You walked around the chair.	You sat near the fire.
John walked across the room.	Mary ran from the dog.
John stood before father.	Mary stood behind mother.
Mr. Smith put on his coat.	The cat jumped from the chair.

I stood between the chair and the table.
I stood between the door and the window.
John sat between father and mother.
Father stood between John and Mary.
You walked from the chair to the table.
You ran from the door to the gate.

COLOR, SIZE, FORM, &c.

The process of teaching color, size, form, possession and numbers will now be considered. In explaining these, some object having the qualities described by the words used must always be placed before the child; otherwise the meaning cannot be made clear to him. He must always learn by seeing, handling, smelling and tasting the objects.

To explain color, make a number of balls of yarn of different colors. These should be of black, white, brown, gray, purple, red, orange, yellow, green, blue, white, violet. Pieces of ribbon, cloth, or sticks painted of these colors, will answer as well. At the printer's, cards of most of the above colors can be had for a trifling sum.

Place one of the balls, say black, before the child, and write the direction—*Touch the black ball*, and proceed as before explained. Continue this with all the colors in turn.

Also, explain the following words of opposite meaning, with suitable objects. The contrast in meaning is a great help towards understanding them: and for this reason first one and then the other should be used:

> hot, cold; hard, soft; wet, dry; clean, dirty; sweet, sour; thick, thin; fat, lean; sharp, dull; new, old; high, low; full, empty; smooth, rough; straight, crooked; wide, narrow; sound, rotten; fragrant, fetid; light, heavy; &c.

Size will now be considered. Get two objects of the same kind, but differing much in size, as stones, potatoes, apples, books, &c., and with these teach the meaning of the words *large* and *small*. Place both before the pupil and direct him to touch one, and give him the proper form of sentence to describe what he has been doing. Do the same with the other, and repeat until the words are understood.

ARITHMETIC.—NUMBERS.

In teaching numbers, get stones, sticks, beans, or marbles, to count with. Then give the following directions, and show the child how to carry them out and express what he has done:

> Put one bean on the table.
> Put two beans on the table.
> Put three beans on the table.

This exercise may be continued until all the numbers up to one hundred have been learned. Let the child learn both the names and the characters used to represent the numbers. Let the teacher himself, as well as other persons, put objects in different places, and teach the child to describe what they do. In this exercise, language as well as numbers are being learned at the same time, as the examples here given will show:

> I put four books on the table.
> I put nine stones in the pail.
> I put fifteen beans under the table.
> You put one stone and seven sticks in the hat.

ADDITION.

To teach addition, put down two beans before the child, and pointing from one to the other, give him the sentence, *One and one are two*, to copy. When this is mastered place one bean at his left hand and two at his right, and let him write, *One and two are three*. Then, with one and three beans, placed in the same way, teach him to write, *One and three are four*. Go on in this way up to *One and ten are eleven*. Keep on until the child can write out this part of the table correctly.

SUBTRACTION.

When we come to subtraction we have simply to place a row of beans before the child, and taking away one or more, give him the proper form in which to express the operation.

Begin by placing two beans before him, and then taking away one, write *One from two leaves one*. So proceed up to *One from eleven leaves ten*. When this is mastered, change the places of the sentences and let the child fill up the blank spaces thus:

> One from six leaves ——.
> One from two leaves ——.
> One from nine leaves ——.

Proceed in this manner until the tables in subtraction are thoroughly mastered.

MULTIPLICATION.

In multiplication the beans are to be arranged in groups containing an equal number. First place one bean before the child, and another a little way from it, and have him write, *Two times one are two*. Then place two beans in each group, and write *Two times two are four*. Next put three beans in each group, and write *Two times three are six.* In this way proceed to *Two times ten are twenty.* As before, finish by changing the places of the sentences and leaving a blank for the pupil to fill up. Teach the remaining tables in the same way.

DIVISION.

In division there may be a little more difficulty, but patience will overcome all. Here the process consists in arranging a row of beans before the child, and then separating it into groups containing the same number.

. Place two beans before the pupil. With both hands separate them and draw each a little to one side. Then write *One is in two twice.* Now separate in the same way a row of four beans, and write *Two is in four twice.* In this manner continue till *Ten is in twenty twice,* has been reached. Change the places of the sentences, and proceed as before described. Finish all the tables in division in this way.

The teaching of fractions is far less difficult than may at first sight appear.

Let there be some apples in the room, and give the child the direction, *Bring me one apple.* Take the apple, and in his sight divide it into two equal parts. Then write the direction, *Bring me one-half of the apple,* explaining the phrase *one-half of the apple,* by pointing to it and then to the object. Then write, *Bring me two halves of the apple.* As in the previous exercises, let the child be practised frequently, until he has mastered this. Show him that *one-half* and ½ mean the same thing.

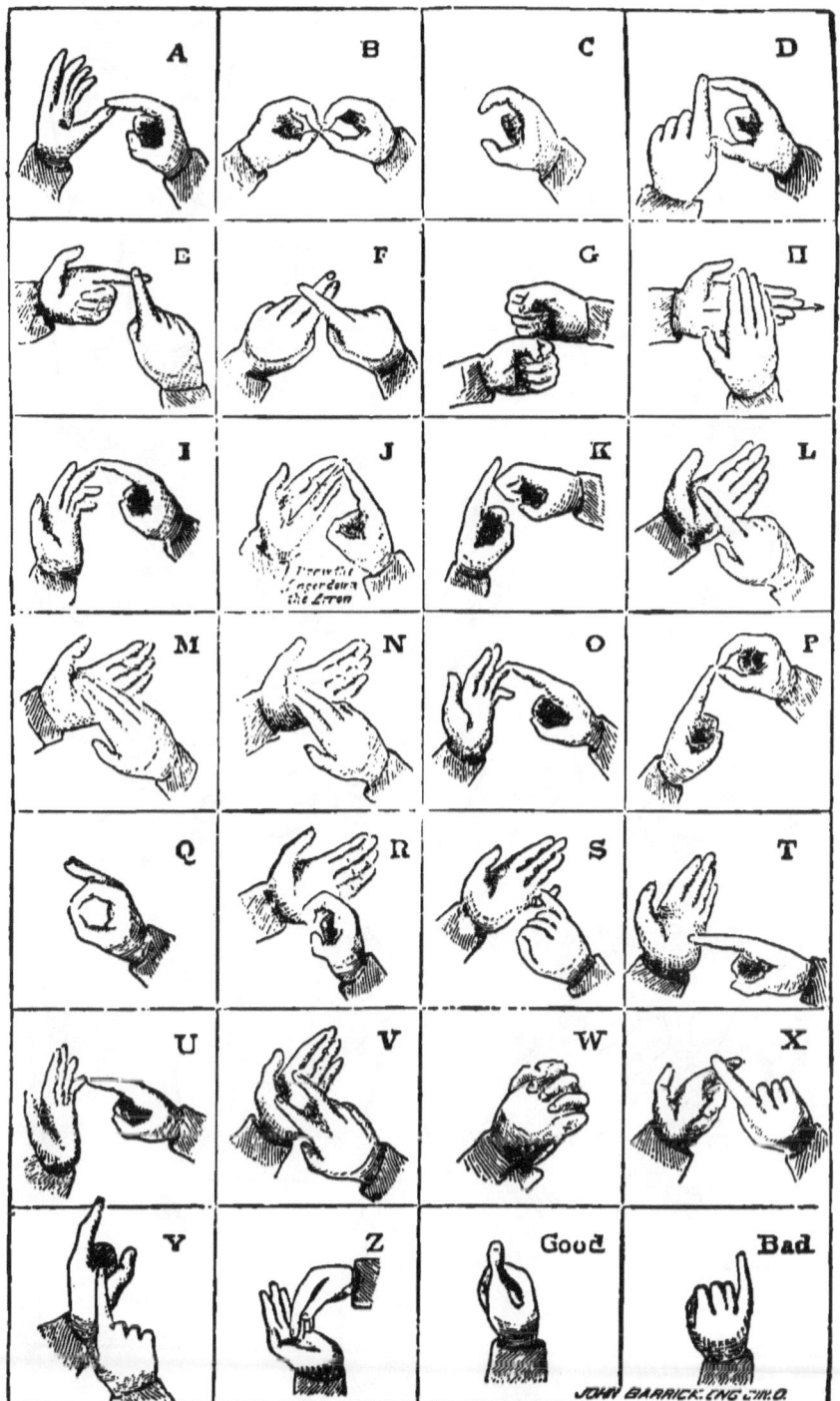

JOHN BARRICK ENG CIN O.

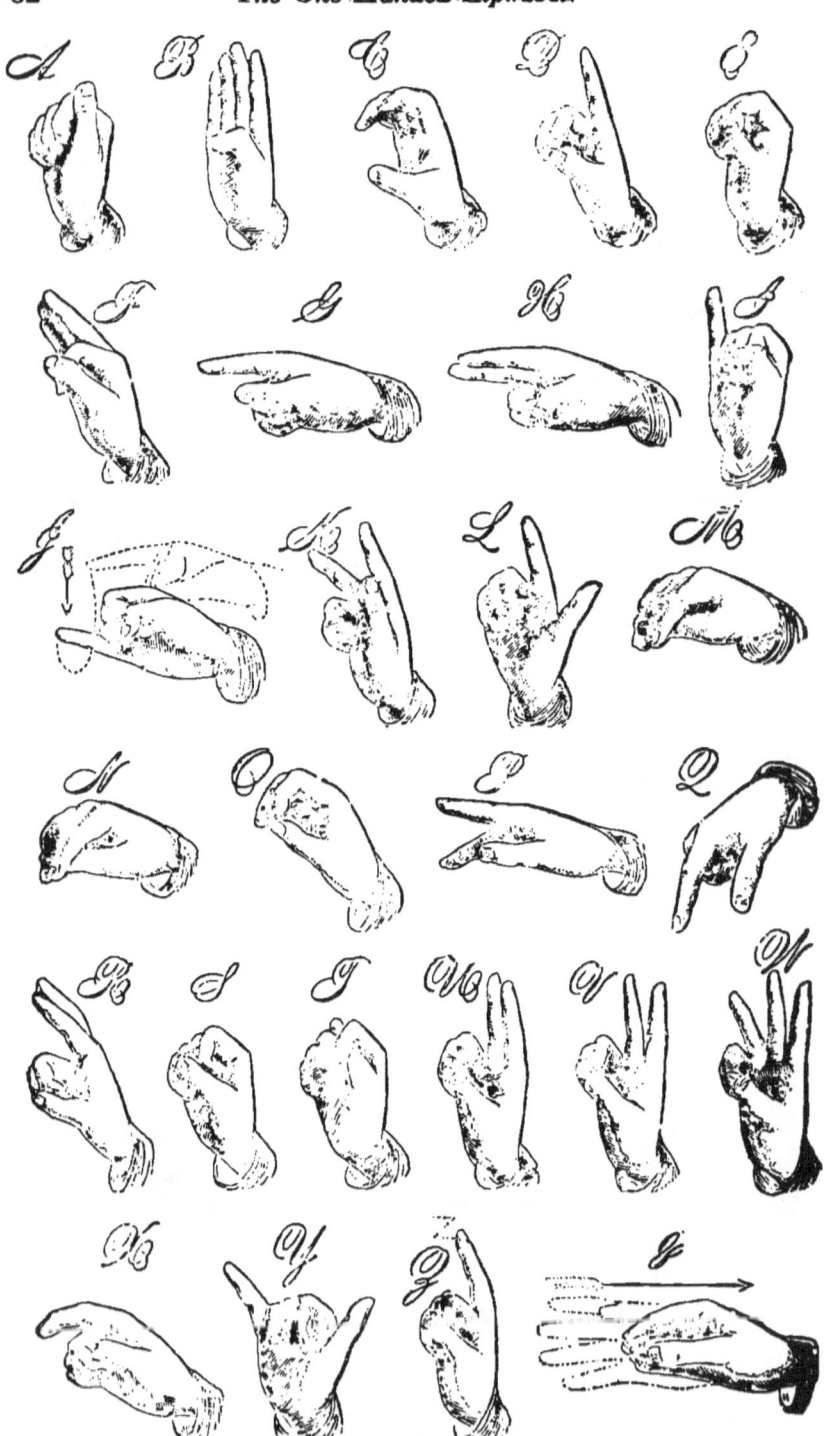